LOST SOULS

LOST SOULS

A Cainsville Novella

KELLEY ARMSTRONG

Illustrations by Xavière Daumarie

SUBTERRANEAN PRESS 2017

First Edition

ISBN
978-1-59606-821-6

Subterranean Press
PO Box 190106
Burton, MI 48519

subterraneanpress.com

PROLOGUE

WHEN ROBERT first saw the young woman, he thought she was a ghost. It was an old story—a woman in white hitchhiking on a lonely road. When someone picks her up, they're directed to a spot near a cemetery, where she promptly disappears.

As he slowed, though, he could see she was very much a creature of flesh and blood. A figure from a very different oft-told story, the sort found in pop songs, a pretty young thing standing in the rain while his car was warm and dry inside.

The girl stood on the gravel shoulder, her thumb out, a magazine over her head to stave off the June rain. The soaked paper sagged, water running down her white sundress, like the Sunday school version of a wet-shirt contest, and he felt a twitch of lust. He also felt his foot press the brake.

When the car stopped, she ran over and opened the door. "Oh, thank you. Thank you!"

She climbed in before he was even fully aware that he'd offered a ride to a stranger on a dark and empty country road. He didn't tell her he'd made a mistake, though. He was too busy noticing the lack of a bra under that wet sundress.

He deserved this. He really deserved this. Sure, he felt a rush of guilt, thinking of Sharon at home making him a late dinner, but it wasn't as if he hoped to run off with a girl he picked up on the roadside. No, he was just going to enjoy the scenery. Nothing wrong with that.

"You okay, mister?" she asked.

Mister? Well, that made him feel old. But he *was* probably twice her age, which he'd peg at about twenty-two. Old enough that he didn't feel like a total perv for ogling her.

He unstuck his eyes from the gaze-magnets under that dress and looked upward. She was a very pretty girl. Like something out of an ad for spring water, sweet and blond and innocent. The kind of girl who, fifty years ago, would have put flowers in her hair and joined a commune and preached free love, having sex with any guy who caught her eye and maybe a few girls too, and—

Down, boy.

"Where are you going?" he asked.

"I'm staying with a friend who lives out here. This guy in the city promised me a ride and then flaked out. I caught a cab, but my money ran out..." She gestured at the roadside with a wry smile. "Right about here. It's only five more miles, and I thought I could walk it, but then the rain started. I stuck out my thumb and hoped I'd get lucky." Her smile broadened. "Which I did."

No, Robert was certain *he* was the one who'd gotten lucky.

"Just tell me when I need to turn off," he said.

"It's about three more miles. You can just drop me at the intersection."

"Two miles from your friend's place?"

She smiled, a sweet and serene smile. "She lives off the beaten path, as they say, and I don't want you going out of your way. Or taking this nice car down those rough roads. The rain is already letting up. Dropping me at the corner will be fine."

"Two miles is a long walk and a short drive. The car will be fine. It has all-wheel drive."

"If you insist…"

"I do."

"Thank you."

Another smile. She went quiet after that, looking out the window. Robert tried to keep his eyes on the road. But, damn, even if all he got at the end of this trip was another sweet thank you, the scenery alone was worth the detour. The phrase "ethereal beauty" kept springing to mind, and he wasn't sure why until he recalled using it in a poem he wrote for Sharon in college.

He'd had no idea what the term meant at the time—he'd been a lovesick boy trying to impress a girl—but the young woman beside him summed up the phrase perfectly. There was a glow about her, with her pale skin and blond hair and white sundress. He imagined what it'd be like to brush the hair from her shoulder, push down that strap, watch the dress slide—

His phone rang through the Bluetooth. As Sharon's name flashed on the screen, the girl looked over.

"Looks like your wife's calling," she said. "Is she expecting you?"

"Wife? No. It's just a coworker."

He hit Ignore. Then he put his left hand down at his side and wriggled off his wedding band. It plunked into the door storage slot. Not that he planned anything untoward. It was just awkward, ogling her while he wore his wedding band. That did make him feel like a perv.

The Bluetooth clicked, and Sharon's voice came on. "Hey, babe—"

He scrambled to stop the message but hit all the wrong buttons as Sharon continued, "Shitty weather out there. Be careful on the back roads. I'll have a drink waiting—"

He disconnected the phone.

"Coworker?" the girl said.

"We…have a thing."

"Ah." Then, "She sounds nice."

She was. More than nice. Robert knew how lucky he was, still happy after almost twenty years of marriage. But happy didn't mean satisfied. Okay, sure, they didn't really have any problems in that area, either. It was just…well, twenty years with one woman was a long time.

He'd never leave Sharon. Not for anyone. But if this girl wanted to give him a little something in payment for the ride, well, he deserved that, didn't he? Cosmic recognition of the fact he worked his ass off, that he was a good husband, a good father…

And your wife?

He gave a start and looked over. The words seemed to come from the girl, but she was staring out the window. That inner voice continued.

And what about Sharon? Hasn't she been all that, too—good worker, wife, mother? What if she picked up some hot young thing by the roadside and—

He shook off the thought. He was just enjoying the scenery. That was all. And if this girl wanted to find a way to thank him— not sex per se, but a little something—then he deserved that for picking her up, giving her a lift, being a gentleman about it.

Gentleman?

Okay, that wasn't the word, but he was acting more respectful than most guys would. He hadn't hit on her, and he wouldn't try to claim any kind of payment, not even a quick feel as he helped her out of the car.

That alone deserves a reward.

Did he detect a note of sarcasm?

"Turn up here," the girl said. "The next right."

He took it, and then she had him make a left, a right, a left... Soon they really were on back roads, at first tar and chip, and then gravel, and he winced every time he heard a stone bounce off the side panels.

Robert drove the regional highway daily, but this wasn't an area he'd ever had reason to enter. It was...desolate. That was the word for it. Part of his architect's brain looked around and saw development potential, one of those clusters of multimillion-dollar homes, an oasis for Chicago's wealthy. But his gut said no, this wasn't the sort of place to raise a family. It just wasn't.

"Are you sure we're going the right way?" he asked, squinting against the night. There wasn't a house in sight, and he was sure they'd gone much more than two miles since leaving the main road.

"It's just up here," the girl said, but her tone added, *I think.* And when he looked over, she was chewing her lip, looking from one window to the next, as if searching for landmarks.

"Maybe we should—" he began.

"Just a little farther. Take the next left."

He did. Watching the odometer, though, the "next left" turned out to be almost two miles away.

"Do you have her address?" He tapped the screen on his car dash. "I can plug it into the GPS."

"It's just up here. The next road will be on the right. Oh, there it is! See?"

He turned right...onto what was little more than a dirt trail.

"You can let me out here if you want," she said when he couldn't suppress a flinch as the tires thunked down into a rut.

He looked at her, white dress glowing in the pale moonlight.

"I'm fine," he said, reminding himself that he knew a good auto body shop if there were any scratches. "I would never leave you out here."

"That's very sweet." She looked up at him with big brown eyes. "I appreciate how kind you've been."

Did he imagine it, or did she lean a little closer when she said that? He watched as her breasts pressed against her bodice, and he adjusted his jacket to cover his reaction.

Perhaps he should *let* her see how much he appreciated the scenery. Nothing wrong with that. Just as long as he kept both hands on the wheel, allowing himself only sidelong glances, being a gentleman. Controlling himself.

He imagined getting to her destination. Her friend's house would be dark, and he'd insist on walking her up, nothing untoward. Just making sure everything was okay. He'd open the passenger door, and she'd turn and be confronted by his obvious interest, right at eye level. He'd pull his jacket shut quickly, act like he hoped she hadn't seen that. She'd smile, biting her lip as she rose. Then she'd lean in and say, in her breathy voice, "You've been so kind. I'm sorry if I've inconvenienced you." And before he could say no, no, that was fine, he'd feel the tug of his zipper and her slender hand sliding inside, warm fingers wrapping around him—

Robert shifted in his seat.

She looked over. "You really can just drop me off. You must have other things to do."

"No, no, I'm fine. Your friend is waiting."

"Actually, she's not home. She's on the night shift, or I'd have called for a lift. I have the house all to myself."

The image flashed again, that darkened house, him opening her car door...

He replayed the fantasy, slower now, embellishing it.

"I think it's just up here," she said, and he jumped from his thoughts. His gaze dropped to the odometer. Twelve miles had passed since he'd last looked at it.

Twelve miles? No, that wasn't possible. It must have been two. He'd misread the starting mileage.

"Just up here, you said?" he asked.

When she didn't answer, he looked over to see her nibbling her lip.

"Miss?" he prompted.

"I…I thought it was but…this doesn't look familiar at all." She shook her head sharply. "No, I'm sure this is— Oh, there! Turn right there."

He did and drove another half mile down a rutted road, trees closing in on both sides. Then there was a clunk, as if the tires had dropped onto softer ground. When he squinted out the windshield, he saw that the road had disappeared. He'd gone right off the end of it.

"No," the girl said. "No."

He looked over to see her eyes glistening with tears.

"I-I was so sure I knew where it was, and now I've made you drive all this way."

"It's fine," he said. "Just fine."

He reached over to squeeze her hand, and she turned to him, her eyes brimming with tears. He wanted to slide his arms around her, pull her against him, *feel* her against him, wordlessly soothe her. Then her hand would brush his crotch, and she'd whisper, "I'm so sorry. Let me make it up to you."

He took a deep breath and pulled back. *Save the rescue fantasy until after you've actually rescued her.*

"I have GPS, remember? I just need your friend's address."

"I-I don't know it."

"Well, then let's just give her a call."

"Can I use your phone?"

"Of course." He hit the dashboard screen to bring up his phone and…

"No service." He took his phone from his pocket and double-checked. Yes, definitely no service.

"It's fine," he said. "We aren't exactly lost in the Ozarks. My GPS will bring up a map, and either you'll recognize your friend's street name or we can drive until I have a signal." He squeezed her hand. "I'll fix this."

Big eyes looked up into his. "Thank you."

He pressed a few buttons on the GPS. It flashed No Satellite Found.

"Well, that's inconvenient," he said with a chuckle. "All-wheel drive to the rescue. I'll back out of here and get us back to civilization and a cell zone."

He put the car into Reverse. The tires spun…and went nowhere. He checked the AWD. The dashboard indicator claimed it was engaged. He put the car in Drive and tapped the gas. The tires spun. Reverse? More spinning.

What the hell?

Robert got out, forgetting the girl now as he walked behind the car. Then he circled to stand in front of it. The tires had sunk maybe an inch or two in the soft ground, but his AWD should be able to pull him out of that.

When was the last time he'd engaged the all-wheel drive? Winter? He barely ever used it then, and to be honest, when he flipped it on in bad weather, it was mostly just to make use of a feature he'd paid extra for. Which meant it could have stopped working long ago, and he'd never know…until he needed it.

He circled the car again. Maybe he could give it a push. Get back on the road. He couldn't have driven more than a foot or two past the…

He stood behind the car, looking at the tracks his tires had made. Tracks through soft earth. Tracks as far as he could see, with no sign of a road.

That wasn't possible. He'd been on a narrow dirt road. He'd seen it.

He strode behind the car, walking as he followed the tracks. Twin tracks that left the road and carved a path through thick brush heading toward a forest.

How the hell—?

He gave his head a shake. Not possible. He was imagining things.

"Are you lost?" the girl said, and he wheeled to see her walking toward him.

"What?" he said.

"You're lost."

"No, I'm fine. I just need to figure out—"

Her fingers pressed to his lips. "You're lost. Poor boy. So terribly lost. But it's not too late. Retrace your steps. See where you went off track. That's always the best thing to do when you're lost, is it not?"

He stared at her, and his mouth opened to brush off her nonsense, but instead he felt himself nodding and saying, "Yes."

"You have forty-eight hours to find your way. If you do not…"

She leaned into his ear and whispered, and when he heard what she whispered, his gut went cold, again ready to say no, what the hell—

"Do you understand?" she asked.

"Yes."

"Good. Forty-eight hours."

She lifted on tiptoes, her lips brushing his. Then she disappeared.

ONE

GABRIEL

GABRIEL WALSH was waiting for a phone call. He would settle for a text. Even an e-mail. But a call was what he wanted. His cell phone, however, was not complying, no matter how harshly he glared at it.

True, Olivia was not due to call until tomorrow. That was what they'd arranged. She was heading back from vacation with Ricky, due to arrive Thursday night or Friday morning. Earlier, he'd sent a message suggesting that it might be more convenient for her to call today. That was his way of saying he wanted to speak to her but had no work-related excuse to do so. As for the idea of just saying so—*Hey, if you're free, give me a shout*—that went too far. Which was exactly how they'd gotten into this predicament in the first place.

A month ago, a car on a dark road, the two of them arguing. She said something about them being friends, an offhand comment. And he'd...

He wasn't sure exactly what he'd done. Made some dismissive noise. A snort. A grunt. A laugh. He'd been hurt and confused, and he'd lashed out and been cruel. Yes, cruel.

KELLEY ARMSTRONG

Then afterward, once the dust settled, their case solved...

When you said we were friends, and I laughed. I was angry. We are. I hope you know that.

How long had it taken him to work up the nerve—and shoulder past his pride—to say those words? Too long. But he'd done it. And he'd watched her squirm. Too little, too late. The problem stayed, and Olivia left.

Not *left*. She went on vacation, and she was heading home now.

When his cell phone rang, he snatched it up. It wasn't Olivia's ringtone, but it could be her, so he grabbed the phone and...

Call display showed a client's number.

Gabriel grunted. Therein lay the problem with giving clients his personal number. They tended to use it.

He let the call go to voicemail and made a mental note to tell Lydia to deliver an update. That's all the message would be. The client looking for news on a legal matter that was of utmost importance to her—one that guaranteed she'd stay on the preferred side of a prison wall—but to Gabriel, it was just another such matter on a calendar filled with them.

When he had news, he would give it. Until then, reassuring a client that he was doing his best to keep her out of jail was ultimately a waste of time. Of course he was doing his best. He was Gabriel Walsh, thirty years old and already one of Chicago's most famous— some might say infamous—defense attorneys. One did not achieve that status through lackluster effort.

He put away his phone and skimmed the day's schedule. Plenty of work. None of it interesting. That's the type of client call he'd prefer. A lead on an interesting case for Olivia when she returned.

I bring you the gift of murder and mayhem, a puzzle to be solved, a mystery to be cracked.

A case for them to investigate together.

Finding that was proving more difficult than one might expect. True, in a city the size of Chicago, there was always murder, always mayhem, but lately it seemed only the pedestrian sort that would induce yawns from his new investigator.

Oh, look, another drive-by shooting.

In desperation, Gabriel had resorted to a tactic he hadn't used since he first hung out his shingle: monitoring the police scanners. He didn't necessarily need a terrible crime. In fact, it would be better if it weren't. Olivia was the daughter of a serial killer, and like Gabriel, she had fae blood—both of which meant she was not particularly altruistic. But she wasn't cold-hearted, either. The ideal case for her was more mind-twisting than gut-wrenching. A puzzle rather than a tragedy.

But the only intriguing case on last night's scanner came from a man who'd reported a disappearing hitchhiker. A preposterous story from someone who failed to recognize a hoary urban legend. Yet that was the part that intrigued Gabriel. He'd picked up enough from the scanner conversation to know the man seemed to be a sober middle-aged professional. Why on earth would he risk his reputation reporting an obviously fabricated story?

Intriguing, yes, but it wouldn't be enough for Olivia. He needed—

"Good morning, Gabriel."

His office door swung open. In walked a man who looked about Olivia's age. Dark hair, worn somewhere between hipster and bohemian. Sharp eyes, sharp cheekbones, sharp chin. He bore a broad grin and two cardboard cups of coffee, the latter of which he deposited on Gabriel's desk, along with a creamer, milk, sugar and sweetener.

"Someday, you're going to tell me how you like your coffee," Patrick said.

"Delivered by my admin assistant." Gabriel shot a glower out the open door.

"Lydia's not there. She slipped out to turn off her car alarm. Seems to be on the fritz."

"You set off her car alarm so you could sneak into my office?"

"I wouldn't need to if you'd tell her that I'm welcome to visit anytime I like." Patrick thumped into a chair. "That would be the wise thing to do, Gabriel. I'm on my best behavior with her, for your sake. That won't last, and then I'll be forced to resort to type."

By "type" he meant fae type. Patrick was a bòcan. Better known as a hobgoblin, though Patrick hated the term. It conjured up images of twisted goblin-like creatures. A bòcan was a fae trickster, and like all tricksters, Patrick had an air of the passive-aggressive about him. Treat him well, and he'd return the favor. Mistreat him—or fail to pay him his perceived due—and one would see his less generous side.

Gabriel wasn't worried about offending Patrick. Following Olivia's example, he'd learned how far he could push while taking advantage of the fact that Patrick liked to be on *their* good side. As for why Patrick wanted to be there, that situation was at the root of Gabriel's fractured relationship with Olivia and therefore not something he wished to consider. Suffice to say the circumstances made Gabriel a valuable ally for Patrick. So he took the coffee and said, "I appreciate you stopping by, Patrick, but I'm very busy—"

"So I see."

"It's eight-thirty in the morning. My appointments begin at nine—"

"Then you have a half an hour for me. And I'm teasing you about not being busy, Gabriel. I know you are. Particularly with Liv jaunting off with biker-boy."

"His name is Ricky. Please show him some respect."

"I find it hard to respect anyone who goes by *Ricky*."

Gabriel walked to the door. "I'll see you out."

"Fine, I won't insult young Mr. Gallagher. You do realize he's the competition, right?"

Gabriel tensed. "Olivia and I are not—"

"I wasn't talking about Liv. But, since that's where your mind went, let's follow it. That conversation is well overdue, and I'm glad to hear you acknowledge that you do see Ricky as a rival in that regard."

"I believe I was saying he is not."

"Because he's no competition for you? Agreed. Ricky and Liv, while a darling couple—"

"I have work to do. If you'll excuse me…"

Patrick sighed. "Fine. We'll drop the subject and move on to the point of my visit."

"There's a point?" Gabriel murmured. "That's new."

"Ouch, you've been hanging around Liv too long. There has been a reason for all my recent visits, Gabriel. We call it socializing."

"To which I do not see a purpose. But you said there was an actual point to this particular visit?"

"I've brought you a case."

"The very thing I do not need, having just said that my roster is full."

"This one's different. This one is interesting."

Gabriel hesitated just a heartbeat. Then he picked up a file folder and leafed through the contents. "Yes, well, given that I have quite enough—"

"You're bored."

"I am far too busy to be bored."

"Nope, you're not. Liv's gone, and you're bored."

"With Olivia gone, I believe the proper word would be *resting*."

"Ha. No, sorry. After she left, I bet you had exactly twelve hours of mild relief that the rollercoaster had stopped. Then boredom settled in. You're missing her, too, but it's easier to say you're bored, so we'll go with that. I have brought you a case. A ghost story."

Gabriel closed the folder and laid his fingertips on it.

"Ah, that got your attention," Patrick said.

"Only because I cannot imagine how a ghost could pay my rates."

Patrick sipped his coffee and settled in his chair. "Picture the scene. It's a dark and stormy night."

"If that's how you start your stories, it's a wonder you sell any books at all."

"It's not how I start them, which you would know if you *read* my books."

"I scarcely have time to eat, let alone read."

"Oh? I seem to recall a boy who would eat while reading. And walk while reading. It's a miracle you survived childhood without getting hit by a car, your nose stuck in some book. You can't tell me you don't read fiction."

"Not the sort you write," Gabriel murmured.

"Ouch."

"If you have a story to tell, please provide me the CliffsNotes version. My first client arrives in fifteen minutes."

"Fine. Dark and stormy night, yada yada. Guy picks up a hitch-hiker by the side of the road and—"

"And she disappears. Whereupon the man returns home to discover his wife drying their wet dog in the microwave, except it isn't a Chihuahua at all, but a giant rat."

"You know your urban legends."

"As should you, given that you are a writer of supernatural fiction and a scholar of folklore. Yes, I heard that story on the police scanner last night. It is remarkable only for its sheer ridiculousness. I suppose she was wearing white, too."

"Actually, yes. But—"

"And asked to be dropped off near a cemetery?"

"I don't think so."

"Then this ghost lacks proper appreciation for the lore. I am disappointed."

"That sounds remarkably like sarcasm."

"Never." Gabriel took the folder to the cabinet and exchanged it for another. "Even if there were a mystery here, Patrick, there is not a case. Not a paying client. Except, perhaps, work for a good divorce attorney."

"Divorce attorney?"

Gabriel set the new file on the desk and opened it. "A middle-aged man in a luxury vehicle picks up a presumably attractive young woman on a rainy night? Drives her well off the beaten track? That's almost a cliché in itself. If he has a wife, she should be in the market for a divorce lawyer, which I am not. I wouldn't say she even requires a particularly good lawyer, considering her husband was foolish enough to report the encounter. That alone suggests—"

"Supernatural forces at work?"

"I was going to say 'abject stupidity.'"

Patrick rose and perched on the desk instead. "You have a point, though. A very good one. Why would he report it? He is married, by the way. And the hitchhiker was young and, as you say, presumably attractive. Any man with a lick of sense would make up some story about getting lost in the rain and leave it at that."

"Which only means he has not a lick of sense."

"He's a partner at one of the city's leading architectural firms. He has his master's in that *plus* an MBA to manage the business end. Two post-grad degrees. Not a stupid man. His wife is a surgeon. Not a stupid woman, and not one who'd fail to miss the implications of his hitchhiker escapade. So we have a mystery. As for the client, that'd be me. This story has sparked a future book plot, and I'd like to hire you to help me with the research."

"Olivia is the investigator."

"Until you hired her, you did all your investigating yourself. You enjoy it."

"What I enjoy is having an actual client, which is about more than money. A case for me must pay well *and* foster my reputation."

"And interest you."

"That's hardly a factor—"

"Liar. You don't need the money. You don't need the rep boost. What you need is what has been lacking for nearly two weeks. Something you've grown very accustomed to having in your life."

Gabriel started leafing through the file. "Olivia will be back in a couple of days."

"Again, I wasn't talking about Liv. Interesting how your mind keeps going there." Patrick held up a hand against Gabriel's protest. "I was going to say that you've grown accustomed to having exciting cases. But, now that you mention it, there is someone who likes this type of case even more than you do."

Gabriel glanced up from the file.

"Ah, there we go," Patrick said. "I have your attention now."

"No, you have less than five minutes of my *time* now."

"Liv comes back in what, two, three days? I'm sure you know the hours, too, but we won't get into that. Point is, she'd love this case. You know she would. Investigating the report of an urban legend? It'd amuse the hell out of her."

"I really don't have time," Gabriel said, but even he could hear the lack of conviction in his voice. He thought of telling Olivia about this case.

Hitchhiking ghost? Seriously?

Yes, it's ridiculous. I know.

Ridiculously awesome. Let me at it.

Patrick hopped off the desk. "When do you finish work?"

"I—"

"Let me rephrase that. When do your office hours conclude, and you begin the portion of the day we call 'quitting time' and you call 'more-work time'?"

"Five, but—"

"Then I will return at five with details. I'll play Liv for you today. I'll gather everything I can find online, and we'll discuss it over dinner. This case isn't going away. I'll do the scut work, and you can have a package ready for Liv when she returns."

TWO

PATRICK

LIV WAS the key. Liv was always the key, and Patrick smacked himself upside the head for not realizing *that* would be the way to get his son on the case.

This wasn't about research. No, it was about father-son bonding time. Thirty years late, to be sure, and yes, it was a little tougher when Gabriel didn't realize he *was* Patrick's son, but that would change soon enough. Liv had figured it out. And she'd been furious. Marvelously, majestically furious. Which should not make Patrick nearly so happy, being the recipient of that fury, but it did because she was furious on Gabriel's behalf.

That was what his son lacked most in his remarkable life: someone firmly and unwaveringly on his side. Patrick himself had played that role, but not in the right way. He realized that now. The silent cheerleader had its place, but his son had never needed that. What he needed was Liv.

Liv hadn't told Gabriel that Patrick was his father. She was protecting him, as always. But Gabriel's parentage could not remain a secret, and as soon as Liv realized Gabriel was in danger of finding out, she'd break it to him herself.

Patrick's job now was to establish enough of a relationship to soften the blow. He'd lost Gabriel before. Lost him as a baby when Seanna stole him away. Lost him as a teen when Seanna took off and Gabriel disappeared onto the streets. Lost him twice; he would not lose him again.

A few weeks ago, Gabriel had come to Patrick. Of his own accord, for the first time ever. Admittedly, it'd been for information—fae lore to help Liv. And that, Patrick realized, was the key to establishing a relationship with Gabriel.

Quid pro quo.

The unwritten motto of the bòcan. Give and take. A proper offering had to be something of value, naturally. What did Gabriel value? He would say money, but that was just the tangible representation of a deeper need for security, to feel he would never again be that teenage boy, alone on the streets.

Or never again be that child who might as well have been alone on the streets, saddled with a mother who expected him to earn his keep picking pockets. Gabriel had suffered that while his father lived in comfort and ease. A father who would see him every few weeks in Cainsville when Seanna dumped Gabriel at her aunt Rose's place. A father who thought talking to the boy—paying attention to him, buying him a soda—was all he needed, really.

Patrick pushed aside the old regrets. There was work to be done. Work that would not undo the damage but which acknowledged that damage had been done.

Patrick walked to the café counter and placed his order. Just a coffee, and not because he needed it, but because it gave him a table to work at and access to the Internet. Also, admittedly, a change of scenery was always welcome. The scenery here was certainly fine, a young barista adding plenty of eye contact to her conversation, taking longer than necessary to serve his coffee, telling him refills were on the house. More than refills were being offered, he suspected, and he appreciated that, even if he was too busy to pursue the flirtation. He put a five in the tip cup in thanks for the flattery of her attention. Quid pro quo.

Coffee obtained. Ego bump achieved. Time to dive into the research trenches. Patrick had a story to construct. A ghost story for his son.

THREE

GABRIEL

THE SUN was dropping when Gabriel arrived at the spot where Robert Lambert's SUV had given up the ghost...in more ways than one, apparently. While it might seem inopportune—reaching the scene just when he'd need a flashlight to examine it—his timing was intentional.

Thirty minutes from now placed him at the exact time of day when Lambert had stood on this spot and seen his passenger disappear. Gabriel sought to reconstruct the scene as precisely as possible. Rain would help, but it had stopped before Lambert reached this point. Despite Patrick's hyperbole, it had not been a dark and stormy night. Simply growing dark after a rather mundane rain shower, according to the report.

"They gave you the police report?" Patrick had said. "I'd have thought the Chicago Police Department wasn't exactly your biggest fan."

True. But this was outside the CPD's jurisdiction. The state police were not terribly fond of him either, but whether city or state,

Gabriel could always find officers and support staff open-minded enough to value monetary reward over petty prejudice.

"You bribed someone for it," Patrick had said.

"A bribe requires subterfuge, which would become tiresome in an extended relationship. I expressed an interest in the case. My contact offered to send me the report. I will pay him for his time. Or, I should say, you will, as the client in this case."

"How much will I pay?"

"You were generous, as one should be with those who devote their lives to keeping our streets safe."

"Again with the sarcasm."

"It's your imagination. That's what comes with being a writer of fiction."

Gabriel hadn't told Patrick that he intended to visit the scene. The bòcan might have tried to accompany him.

Gabriel looked back at his Jag, parked on the road over a hundred feet away. There was no way he could have driven it back here. He wasn't even sure how Lambert's SUV had managed it.

As he bent to examine the tire tracks, his phone sounded with a tone that had him scrambling to answer, imagining the greeting, as familiar and jaunty as that ring, a singsong "Hey, it's me."

Or that's what he used to get. Now, Olivia's, "Hey," thudded between them, leaden and dull.

"Got your message," she continued. "This isn't too late, is it?"

"Of course not."

"Good. Sorry I didn't call sooner. Long day of riding. Ricky needs to be home by the weekend, and we were already running behind from that thing in Cape Breton."

That thing.

An adventure Gabriel had missed.

He felt a twinge, which he suspected strongly resembled the emotional reaction of a child being reminded of a birthday party to which he had not received an invitation. A new sensation for him. Not because he'd ever been invited to parties, but because he'd never given a damn. Now he did. He'd missed an adventure, and while he could hardly be expected to join them a thousand miles away, it illogically felt the same. A very uncomfortable sensation. Which summed up emotional responses in general.

"Gabriel?"

"Yes, I lost the connection for a moment. I'm out of doors. Pursuing a new case."

Oh? Something new? Something fun?

She would say the last with a lilt in her voice, teasing, almost self-mocking, acknowledging her own predilection for adventure and finding it somewhat childish.

He waited...and Olivia said nothing. Now he was the one prompting her, as if he had indeed lost the connection.

"I'm here," she said. "So, is this a bad time, then?"

He picked his way over the uneven ground. "Not at all. In fact—" The words caught in his throat. He shouldn't tell her about the case. Shouldn't risk admitting that he thought she'd find it interesting, only to discover he was mistaken and look foolish.

Which was how he'd gotten himself into trouble, wasn't it? Hubris. Pride. Fear of humiliation. Like acknowledging that one considers a person a friend only to have that person laugh in your face.

"This case might..." he said. "That is, it seems..."

Get the words out. Tell her it's interesting.

"It's somewhat intriguing," he said finally.

Well, that's close.

He gave Olivia a brief summary.

"A hitchhiking ghost?" she said when he finished. And her tone was not what he'd hoped for. Not at all. "I know you aren't exactly a pop-culture junkie, Gabriel, but that's—"

"An urban legend."

A soft chuckle, more Olivia-like. "You know your modern folklore, then. Good."

"Which is what I found mildly intriguing."

He went on to explain more of the circumstances.

When he finished, she said, "So this seemingly bright professional, who has not completely lost his marbles, actually calls the cops and says he picked up a disappearing hitchhiker? That *is* weird."

Gabriel exhaled. "There's more. Patrick compiled—"

"Patrick?"

"He's the one who brought this to my attention. For book research, apparently."

"*Patrick* brought this to you."

Olivia's tone hardened. She had issues with Patrick, ones that Gabriel couldn't quite comprehend. She didn't appreciate the fact that they'd had to uncover the secrets of Cainsville—the truth about the fae—on their own. Of the elders, though, she blamed Patrick the most. Perhaps because he'd been the most outwardly helpful. She'd trusted Patrick, and he'd betrayed that trust, and really, after dealing with Gabriel, she had quite enough betrayals and not nearly enough trustworthy allies.

"He's been stopping by ever since I left, hasn't he?" she said.

"Yes, and I realize he brought me this case because it provides an excuse to get to know me better. Wriggling into my good graces. Which would be so much more productive if I had any."

She sputtered a laugh at that, and he could imagine her relaxing.

"True enough," she said. "So, in the meantime, if he's intent on currying favor, you might as well fleece him for it. I presume he's paying for this research?"

"Silly question."

That got a real laugh from her, and now *he* relaxed.

Gabriel continued, "He's paying me to investigate an intriguing case, one that provides a break from the rather dull caseload we're dealing with."

"Fair enough."

"And you'll be home in a couple of days, so if you find it interesting..."

"It is definitely weird."

"Weird good? Or just weird?"

She chuckled. "Weird is always good."

The last bit of tension drained from his shoulders. "Then, if you have a moment, I'd like to get your opinion on one particular bit of weirdness."

"Go for it."

"I'm sending a photo. Let me know when you have it."

A moment later, she said, "Tire tracks through thick brush. Is that where he drove?"

"It is. The road curved, and Lambert kept going. Driving a luxury SUV."

"Make and model?"

He told her, and she said, "Yikes. That baby is not made for off-roading. Especially through that brush. I'd hate to see his vehicle."

"It's quite scratched, according to the report."

"I hope you didn't drive the Jag in there."

"Certainly not. The question is, why did he drive in here? *How* did he? I can understand missing the turn, given the darkness and the rural setting, but he drove through a hundred feet of brush without realizing he'd left the road."

"Yeah, that's not possible. I've done off-roading. I remember hearing the suspension hitting the ground and the trees scraping the sides. Vehicular sadism. On a car like that, it should be a criminal offense."

"And from what you're suggesting, 'I didn't notice' would not be a viable line of defense."

"Not unless you could manage to convince a jury that it was still raining. Like a torrential downpour. Or that there was a nearby airfield that covered the sound."

"There isn't. It's the same time of evening, and it sounds like this…" He held out the phone.

"Yeah, no defense there. Is it possible he fell asleep at the wheel?"

"My research suggests this particular vehicle is equipped with features that should have alerted him if that happened. While they could malfunction, that would mean not only a technical failure but a man who slept through a very rough ride while dreaming that he picked up a hitchhiker. And, given that the only reason he left the highway was to drop her off, and then he drove almost an hour from there…"

"That's a whole new level of sleepwalking."

"Also, that hour itself is interesting. His passenger claimed her friend lived only a few miles off the regional highway. Yet, while he said it seemed farther, he was shocked to realize he'd gone nearly thirty miles. He did say that at one point, while tracking the odometer, he seemed to have traveled twelve miles in a few minutes and thought he must have mistaken the initial reading."

"Time lapse, then. Which is more commonly something people report with alien encounters." She paused. "Really hope this isn't aliens."

"There's no such thing as aliens. Or ghosts. Or fairies."

"Don't we wish. I'm drawing the line at aliens, though. I do think I've heard of time distortion in ghost stories. Not that I'm jumping to that conclusion yet. What else have you got?"

He told her what Patrick had uncovered: a pattern of similar reports in the region, stretching back for decades. Gabriel didn't have details. As eager as Patrick had been to provide the stories, Gabriel wanted facts, which he would use to find commonalities and connections before he dug deeper.

The facts were this: in the past fifty years, twenty-three people had reported picking up a hitchhiking "woman in white." That meant twenty-three had filed a police report or gone to the newspapers with their story. Online, Patrick had found many more who'd claimed to have seen the woman or knew a "friend of a friend" who had. Most of those could be dismissed as attention-seeking. Even some of the actual reports could be dismissed on the same basis. That still left a sizable number.

The dates were also of interest. Seven reports had been made in the last two years, meaning almost one-third fell within four percent of the time frame.

"Which does not mean increased occurrences," he said to Olivia. "It's more likely increased awareness. Reports causing more people to step forward."

"Who are either making false reports or are emboldened by the others and coming forward to give their stories. That doesn't explain this Lambert guy—he reported it right away, didn't he?"

"Yes. He walked until he had cell service and called the police."

"Which is weird. Especially when you had cell service in the same spot. I suppose it could be a different provider but... Still seems weird. Are you going to talk to him?"

"I am."

"Anything you'd like me to do?"

Just come home.

"Nothing that will delay your return, as I know Don needs Ricky back. The case will be here for you, if you want it."

FOUR

$\mathcal{G}$ABRIEL

AFTER HIS call with Olivia, Gabriel took a moment.

Take a moment.

A favorite phrase of his, as Olivia had discovered. When a client started to become overwrought—as they were wont to do when facing life in prison—he would tell them to take a moment. He used to say the same to Olivia in her moments of emotional turmoil.

Take a moment.

Clients appreciated this, a gesture of kindness and consideration from a man who seemed incapable of either. Proof that Gabriel was not nearly as cold and detached as he appeared.

Olivia knew better. She'd figured it out from the start.

Do me a favor? Erase those words from your vocabulary. At least with me.

"Take a moment" wasn't a thoughtful invitation but an impatient "get it over with." Work past this inconvenient emotional turmoil so we may return to the business at hand.

Right now, Gabriel was taking a moment, not to recover emotional equilibrium, but to enjoy the recovery of it. Olivia was pleased with the case. She was heading home. She seemed happy about that, ready to start work without hesitation.

He'd feared that in her two weeks away, she would decide not to return to work for him. She could easily go back to waiting tables at the Cainsville diner, and in a few months, her twenty-fifth birthday would bring a multimillion-dollar trust fund from her adoptive family. She didn't need the job he'd given her.

And it's not as if she'd have any reason to regret taking it…

Gabriel rolled his shoulders, sloughing off that damnable voice. Gwynn's voice. An unwanted reminder of so many things. Particularly unwelcome when it spoke the truth. After Gabriel's spat with Olivia—

Spat? Is that what you'd call it?

All right, after he betrayed Olivia's trust—again—he'd told her not to come into work. That had been petty. Bratty, even. Selfish and immature, exercising control in the only way he could.

I am displeased, and so I will hold your job hostage.

The job you love.

The job you don't actually need.

Misplayed. Terribly and shamefully misplayed. He'd let his emotions run roughshod over his common sense. Unforgivable.

Take a moment.

Good advice, even for someone who did not normally suffer from emotional turmoil. No, *especially* for someone who didn't normally suffer from it…and therefore lacked the tools to deal with it.

Gabriel leaned back against a tree and closed his eyes to recover his equilibrium.

Olivia was fine. She was happy with the case. She was coming home.

Listing the positives. The reassurances. An old remedy to cure old anxieties, ones that didn't stay as firmly in the past as he'd like. It'd been over a decade since he'd left the streets, yet he would still lie in bed, waking from a memory, and mentally list his security blankets.

Gun taped under the dresser. Knife under the drawer. Cash under the bed.

I have enough money. I have enough food. I am big enough and strong enough and successful enough that no one and nothing can threaten me.

His mind tripped back to a time when his security blankets had been far more threadbare, *worked* threadbare by him constantly sorting them in his mind, pulling them out to remind himself that his situation was not as dire as it seemed.

A hundred dollars in my shoe. Another thirty in my pocket. Two dented cans of stew and three of Coke in my backpack. A school to attend. No one there is suspicious. I'm just another quiet student, keeps to himself, his mother sick at home. A good student who doesn't cause trouble, so there's no need to dig deeper and discover he doesn't have a home, doesn't have a mother. Not anymore, which is just as well.

Yes, add that to the list of positives.

Seanna is gone.

"Are you lost?" The voice sounds in his memory, and Gabriel surfaces in it, the closest he ever comes to dreaming: replaying old memories.

This memory came from a time not long after Seanna disappeared. A time when Gabriel had begun to realize her departure was not as positive as it seemed. At least with Seanna around, he'd had shelter. Now the landlord had figured out rent wasn't forthcoming... nor were the sexual favors his mother often paid in exchange.

It'd also been growing harder to fool Rose. Gabriel had been taking taxis to Cainsville—saying Seanna dropped him off on Main Street—but that cost far too much to do often, and when he called with excuses, Rose got suspicious.

He'd held out until school ended for the summer. Then he took off. Now he needed to find a place where he could squat long term, so he could re-enroll in a new school for September. Searching for a place made him realize how unprepared he really was. Weak, soft, sheltered even.

However bad things had gotten with Seanna, he'd never spent more than a night or two on his own, staying in a house where the occupants had gone on vacation and not bothered with more than rudimentary security. But he couldn't expect to find a house left vacant for months. Nor could he pickpocket enough to rent a room. As for just accepting transiency and quitting school, that wasn't an option. Seanna had stolen enough from him. She wasn't taking his future.

What Gabriel needed was a neighborhood with enough bolt-holes that he could rotate among them. Searching for that, though, proved how ill-equipped he was. Like a boy from the countryside thinking rural life prepared him for a year in the Alaskan wilderness. He'd been wandering from neighborhood to neighborhood, losing track of landmarks as night fell and—

"Are you lost?" the voice asked again.

A woman stepped from the ruined doorway of the empty building he'd been picking through.

"No," he said. "I'm fine."

"You seem lost."

She was young, perhaps in her early twenties. Light brown hair worn long and loose. Dressed in a blouse and long skirt. No visible purse or pockets, which meant she'd make a poor target for his light fingers.

"Are you lost?" she repeated.

He pulled himself upright. He was tall for his age, skinny but learning to compensate for that through bulky clothing, a broad stance and squared shoulders. He surreptitiously knocked mortar dust from his sweater.

"I am conducting an examination of local architecture as a summer project," he said. "This is an excellent example of the period."

Her lips twitched. "That sounds very proper. All grown up, are you, boy?"

He tensed at the lilting mockery in her voice. Her phrasing seemed odd coming from someone so young. The kind of thing an old man might say. *Well, don't you speak all fancy, boy.*

Gabriel's diction was one of the few things for which he could thank Seanna. She might not even have graduated high school herself, but she'd had no patience with baby talk. He'd also discovered an advantage to speaking above his age: it elevated him above his station as well. Like a chimney sweep with an Oxford accent. He might have a drug-addled part-time prostitute, full-time con artist for a mother, but he didn't sound as if he did.

"If this is your building, I apologize," he said. "I'll leave now."

"And where will you go?" she said as he headed for the door. "Where will you stay?"

He hoped he didn't look too surprised at that. He had never been recognized as a street kid before. He had a rough look to him, but he overcame it with careful attention to dress and posture and grooming.

"I will go home, of course. Now, if you'll excuse me..."

Her lips curved, a smile somewhere between pity and mockery, and he wasn't sure which jabbed harder. He fixed her with a steady gaze. That usually did it—people found his eyes unsettling. Too pale a blue. Spooky, kids said, when they thought he couldn't hear them.

The woman only looked him straight in the eye and said, "Oh my, you *are* lost, aren't you?"

"You are mistaken," he said and brushed past her.

As he headed through the building, she followed, saying, "I'm sorry if I offended you, child."

Child? That was even worse than *boy*.

"I only want to help you find your way," she continued.

"I know my way, thank you."

"Do you?"

Yes, he did. Seanna's disappearance required a slight detour in his life's plan, but it changed nothing. He would adapt. He would persevere. High school. College. Law school. Success.

Money. Security. Peace.

"I know my way," he said again.

"Is it the right way?"

"Yes."

"Are you certain?"

He turned and fixed her with that look again. "Quite certain, and while I appreciate your concern—"

She touched his arm, and he jumped. An instinctive reaction to being touched, one that he'd learned to overcome. Failing now proved his agitation.

Go. Just go now.

"Let me show you the way out," she said.

"It's right there." He nodded toward a broken window.

"I can show you a better way. Put you on the right track."

He let out a snort that made *her* give a start. "Oh, now I see."

"See what?"

"Child services? Social worker? Or is it religion? I do hope it's not religion. That's passé. Please tell me it's a cult. I have always wanted to be recruited by a cult."

She stared as if he'd begun speaking in tongues. Again, nothing new. Sarcasm, he'd learned, was not something people expected from him. He just didn't seem the type.

"What are you?" she asked.

"A teenage boy who is not nearly as gullible as you seem to think. Whatever you are selling, I do not wish to purchase. Find easier prey."

With that, he'd walked off. Walked more quickly than he'd liked. More unsettled than he'd liked, and while he told himself he'd been right—she was some social worker, some religious do-gooder—his sixth sense for trouble kept his feet moving as fast as they'd take him, out of that building and onto the next city bus, heading for parts unknown. Away from her. That was all that mattered.

Are you lost?

Gabriel started awake, his feet scrabbling against the ground as he narrowly avoided landing flat on his ass. Which was what happened when one drifted off to sleep while leaning on a tree. He blinked and gave himself a shake.

You're lost.

The voice seemed to echo from his memory, leaching into the real world, and he growled under his breath as he straightened.

He looked around. Was there anything else he needed to do here? He'd examined the tire tracks, which proved that Lambert had driven his SUV through thick brush before getting stuck—

Yes, getting stuck.

You're lost.

Gabriel pushed his mind back on course. Not as simple as it usually was. Even as he bent to examine the end of the tracks, he kept hearing that voice from his past, prodding at him.

Yes, yes, I understand. Lambert got himself lost. It is a poor analogy. Poor indeed.

He took photographs of the tire treads and then poked at them to determine some rough measurement of depth. A couple of inches? No sign that Lambert had struck anything that made the SUV stop. Simply wet ground, and if his all-wheel drive had left him mired in two inches of mud, he ought to demand a refund on the option.

Lambert had postulated a malfunctioning system, but the police report said his mechanic found no sign of that. The car had simply gotten stuck. In two inches of mud.

Gabriel looked around. As he turned, he caught a glimpse of movement to his left and spun, his eyes narrowing against the darkness.

It was night now. A check of his phone said an hour had passed. Lambert mentioned time shifts.

No, Gabriel had fallen asleep. Standing up. While his teen years meant he'd perfected the ability to sleep anywhere, that did seem extreme.

He squinted into the night. Again, he caught a glimmer of movement just beyond his field of vision, making him spin and—

A pale figure darted through the trees.

"Who's there?" he said.

His voice echoed in the silence. He strode forward and pushed aside a bush to see a pale birch tree, the branches and leaves waving in the breeze.

He shook his head and started to turn back.

You're lost.

Gabriel squeezed the bridge of his nose. A soft sigh echoed through the night. He didn't even look up. The wind in the trees. A white birch in the shadows. A voice from his past. All adding up to nothing more than his own nerves, which was, yes, unnerving. Not like him at all. He felt unsettled.

Unsettled.

His phone rang. He snatched it out to see the name of the client from this morning, the one whose call he'd forgotten to have Lydia return. One last glance around at the forest, and then he answered the phone as he strode back to his car.

FIVE

GABRIEL

WHEN GABRIEL walked into Lambert's office, he found the architect working on two computers, desktop and laptop, switching from one to the other. Which seemed odd. Not that Gabriel failed to respect efficient multitasking, but from his vantage point, he could see the laptop screen, which showed what looked like a vacation-planning website, with a young couple splashing through the surf under the heading "Summer Sand Sale!"

Seeing that advertisement, Gabriel flashed back to the night with Olivia before everything went wrong. They'd just solved the crimes for which her parents had spent the last twenty years in prison. Bittersweet victory, which they'd celebrated on the shores of Lake Michigan, walking along the surf and then drinking wine and talking about dreams and fancies. One perfect night, perfectly destroyed when—

"Who the hell are you?" Lambert said, scrambling to his feet. The architect brushed a hand through his hair. "I mean, I'm afraid I'm not taking new clients. I'm sorry my receptionist wasn't at her desk to receive you."

"She was."

"Then how…"

Lambert paused. Taking a moment. He looked as if he could use one. Or twenty. He definitely looked as if he could use the vacation displayed on his laptop. Gabriel had met with clients who appeared less harried and exhausted after a weekend in lockup.

The firm's website photo showed Lambert as a fit and handsome forty-five-year-old, the very picture of calm and confident professionalism. The man in front of Gabriel looked as if he hadn't even changed his clothing in days. His hands shook so badly Gabriel would presume drug withdrawal if he didn't trust the state police enough to know they wouldn't have missed the signs.

"Your receptionist seemed under the mistaken impression that I'm with the police," Gabriel said. "I merely said I needed to speak to you about Monday night."

Lambert winced. "You're a reporter, aren't you?"

Gabriel arched one brow and cast a pointed look down at his suit, which would not belong to any member of the fourth estate lacking a trust fund the size of Olivia's…and likely not even then, given the fashion sense of the journalists he knew.

"No," he said slowly. "I am a lawyer, representing—"

"Sharon." Lambert exhaled his wife's name. "She contacted a divorce lawyer."

"No, but given the circumstances, I can see where you'd be concerned about that."

Lambert flushed. "It's a misunderstanding. It was raining, and this girl was hitchhiking. I wanted to help."

"I'm sure you did," Gabriel murmured. "However, I have to wonder why you would tell your wife. Why you'd tell anyone."

Panic flashed behind Lambert's eyes. He opened his mouth. Closed it. Inhaled and straightened, as if this really was such an obvious question it didn't require a response.

"I had to warn them, didn't I? Report the girl missing?"

"The girl disappeared into thin air. That's what you told—"

"I was mistaken. People don't vanish. Not outside cheap magic shows." A forced hearty laugh. "The police misunderstood."

"You told them *multiple* times—"

"They misunderstood. I meant that she wandered off into the forest while I was checking the car. I was concerned. Understandably concerned."

"About that forest... You drove several hundred feet off the road, through thick brush, in a very expensive vehicle."

"It's an SUV. It's meant for that. I was just driving the girl home."

"She lives in the forest?"

Sweat beaded on Lambert's temple. "I mistakenly believed it was a narrow road. That's what she said. It wasn't until I got stuck that I realized otherwise."

"You also reported that you believed you'd driven no more than ten miles off the regional highway when, in fact, you went more than thirty."

"I lost track of time. She was a very good conversationalist."

"What did you talk about?"

The drop of sweat slid down Lambert's jaw. At this point, all he had to say was that his conversation was none of Gabriel's business. But human nature hungered for confession.

"You've been asked to keep this quiet, haven't you?" Gabriel said. "Asked—strongly—to recant your story. By your partners in this firm."

"No, of course not." A nervous glance toward the door. "Why would you say that?"

"Don't insult my intelligence, Mr. Lambert. I'm not a reporter. I'm a servant of the law"—roughly speaking—"trying to uncover the truth with no interest in embarrassing anyone. You claim to have seen a ghost. I am not disputing that claim. I simply wish to establish facts, and lying to me will not help your case."

"Case?"

A rap at the door. A portly, graying man stuck his head in. "Everything all right, Robert?"

"Yes," Gabriel said. "I'm here to discuss the woman Mr. Lambert encountered Monday evening. The one who went missing. We may have a lead on her, and I thought he should know."

"A lead? Excellent. Sorry to have interrupted, then."

The door closed, and Lambert exhaled. "Thank you."

"No need. As I said, I'm not interested in exposing you to ridicule. Now, let's back up. Why did you report this to the police?"

"I-I don't know."

Gabriel eyed the man. Noted the widening of his eyes. The tremble in his jowl. The jaw working until he blurted, "I honestly don't know. I just called. I told my story, and it wasn't until hours later that I realized how ridiculous it sounded. It just—it made sense at the time. Like reporting that I'd been mugged. Why wouldn't I?" A sharp laugh. "Because I claimed to have seen a ghost? Claimed not to know how I ended up hundreds of feet off the road? Said I'd experienced some sci-fi time lapse? I know how crazy all that sounds now, but at the time, it made perfect sense."

Lambert took quick, short breaths, leaning against his desk, shuddering with the relief of his confession.

"Maybe I do need a psych eval," he said finally.

"I believe a more thorough drug test might have been more useful."

Lambert looked up. "If you're implying—"

"It would seem clear to me that you were suffering from the effects of a drug you didn't realize you'd ingested. That this girl injected you with something."

Lambert collapsed back into his chair. "Yes, that's it. That must be it."

While this was one possible explanation, the police would have been looking for signs of drug consumption. So why offer Lambert a rational explanation? Because it was easily done. Lambert's state of mind was not Gabriel's concern, but there wasn't any reason *not* to offer an explanation that would put the architect at ease.

Olivia would be pleased.

That was what Gabriel thought. Not that he was glad he could ease Lambert's mind, but that it would please Olivia.

See, I am capable of considering others.

Just as long as it's not terribly inconvenient to do so.

Gabriel motioned at the laptop. "I presume those are vacation plans for you and your wife?"

Again, Lambert could say it was none of Gabriel's business, but that peck of altruism had bought a bushel of goodwill, and Gabriel could see that in Lambert's face, as open and relaxed as if he'd downed three shots of Scotch.

Lambert nodded. "I have to fix this."

"Fix the situation with your wife."

Lambert's hands started to tremble again, that panicked look returning as he said, "I'm running out of time."

"Time?"

"Forty-eight hours," Lambert murmured. "I only have forty-eight hours."

"Until what?"

Lambert's head jerked up. "Hmm?"

"You said you only had forty-eight hours. Until what?"

Lambert's brow creased, as if Gabriel's words sounded famil-iar, but he couldn't place them. "I'm sorry. I don't know what you mean." He checked his watch, and he pulled over his laptop. "I really need to get back to work."

"You mean you need to get back to booking that vacation."

"Yes, I'm running out of time." Lambert blinked, seeming con-fused. "For the sale. I'm running out of time for the sale."

"I see."

"I lost my way. I need to get back on track."

The hairs on Gabriel's neck rose. "Back on track?"

That look again from Lambert. The one that made Gabriel feel as if he were working from a different script in this scene.

"What?" Lambert said.

"You said you'd lost your way and needed to get back on track."

More confused blinking, and Gabriel imagined Lambert peer-ing at his script, wondering where that dialogue came from.

"Back on track for work," he said, quickly and firmly resolving the matter. "I need to get back to work, and I'm afraid I must ask you to let me do that. Good day, Mr.... What did you say your name was again?"

Gabriel turned and walked out of Lambert's office.

SIX

PATRICK

PATRICK KNEW his son did not play well with others. That wasn't a trait he'd learned from either parent, but rather—he feared—from experience.

Seanna might have liked to surround herself with friends and admirers—or, as she'd call them, marks and dupes—but Patrick suspected she'd have seen no reason to encourage her son's socialization. In fact, she'd have likely discouraged him from making friends because it might prove inconvenient to her. She wouldn't want kids snooping around, getting underfoot, scaring off those dupes and marks, and possibly showing her young son that pickpocketing and petty theft were not skills most parents taught their offspring.

So Gabriel did not play well with others. He lived alone. Started his own law firm straight out of school. Only hired Lydia when doing administrative work began to impede his earning potential. But he didn't work *with* Lydia. No one earned that spot until Gabriel had met a certain former socialite with serial killer parents.

With Liv away, Patrick had hoped Gabriel missed the experience of working closely with another person. Another person like Liv—clever enough, resourceful enough and devious enough to keep up with Gabriel. A person like Patrick.

Evidently not.

Patrick had spent most of yesterday composing a ghost story for his son. Supplementing what he found online. Adjusting facts. Photoshopping articles to better support the story he wished to tell.

It was, truly, a creative masterpiece. And Gabriel wanted nothing to do with it. He'd refused the file of carefully curated—and constructed—evidence.

Just the facts, sir. Give me the facts, and I'll research them on my own.

Which meant that, at any moment, his son was going to discover his "case" was nothing more than a conveniently timed example of an urban legend in action.

Worse, Patrick had triggered Liv's suspicions. She'd called last night to find out what he was up to, knowing there was no way in hell he needed this for book research. She suspected he was trying to wriggle into his son's good graces while she was away, unable to intervene.

She'd also inadvertently tipped him off to Gabriel's night-time visit to the scene. Which meant Gabriel was actively investigating. Without Patrick. Robbing him of the opportunity even to prepare special effects for his visit.

Now Gabriel was interviewing Robert Lambert. Alone. Patrick had called for an update, and Gabriel had said he was "working the case" and, when pressed, admitted he'd be conducting interviews today. While he hadn't said *whom* he planned to interview, it didn't take keen deductive reasoning to realize the top spot would go to the guy whose claim started this investigation.

So Patrick had set up shop in yet another coffee house, this one right across from the architect's office building. He didn't even need to watch out the window. When Gabriel arrived, Patrick noticed— saw the movement in the crowded sidewalk as it cleared. Gabriel had that effect on people. Even those who wouldn't normally clear the way for a guy in an expensive suit changed their minds after one look at Gabriel. Six foot four. Built like a linebacker. With a face better suited to the kind of guy who'd pick you up, put you against the wall and say his boss expected payment *now*.

Gabriel himself never seemed to notice the parting of the tide, too intent on his destination. Patrick watched him walk into Lambert's building. Then he packed away his laptop and went outside to wait.

SEVEN

GABRIEL

I LOST my way.

I need to get back on track.

On their own, those words wouldn't have done more than unsettle Gabriel, as they echoed the very memory he'd revisited the night before. He would analyze that at a more appropriate time and consider the likelihood it was a coincidence. Most people would say it was. To presume otherwise indicated the sort of thinking that allowed his great-aunt, Rose, to flourish as a psychic. People like to see connections in coincidence—it's a way to imagine control in chaos. But while Rose might take advantage of magical thinking, she *did* have the sight, a gift of their fae blood. So Gabriel knew better than to automatically reject anything beyond the normal realm of possibility. He suspected it was unlikely that he'd just happened to relive that particular memory in the very place where he'd been investigating a man who now repeated almost the same words.

The location had prompted Gabriel's memory for a reason. That, however, could be dealt with later. What kept those words cycling through his head was the rest of it. Lambert speaking without realizing what he was saying. Lambert frantically trying to "fix" his marriage. Talking about having forty-eight hours to do it. Not knowing why he'd been compelled to report the story to the police.

Compelled.

An interesting word.

A fae word.

Compulsion.

As Gabriel stepped from the office building, someone moved into his path. Which struck him as odd. People were normally so much better about getting in the way of others.

Then he saw who it was.

"Patrick."

"Looks like you beat me to it."

Gabriel arched his brows as he steered past the bòcan.

"I was going to interview Lambert for you," Patrick said, hurrying to keep up. "Save you some time."

"No, that would have doubled the work. When I say I am conducting interviews, it is not a hint for you to do them yourself."

"Well, since I'm here, why don't we grab a coffee—"

"I've had enough caffeine for today."

"I meant we could talk."

"No need. I will update you when I have…" Gabriel slowed as he remembered what he'd been thinking before Patrick waylaid him. *Fae compulsion.* "Actually, I would like to speak, though briefly. I have a full schedule."

"Have you eaten lunch?"

"No, nor do I plan to." Gabriel spotted a coffee shop across the road. "I'll have something there while we speak."

"Not that one," Patrick said quickly. "Health violations. I see one farther down."

Gabriel checked his watch.

"It's a sixty-second walk, Gabriel. Thirty at your speed."

"All right. I can spare fifteen minutes."

"How about twenty?"

"I bill in fifteen-minute increments. Twenty would double the price."

"You're charging me for coffee?"

"Of course not. You can buy your own."

⟿

"THAT'S not lunch, Gabriel," Patrick said as they took seats. "It's not even solid food."

"It's a mocha, which provides an efficient way to replenish my blood sugar while I talk."

"Have you ever had a mocha?"

"No, but Olivia is fond of them." Gabriel took a sip.

"Yeah…" Patrick said as Gabriel struggled not to make a face. "A little sweet? Learning to like mochas isn't going to help you get back with Liv. If you want my advice—"

"Preferably not." Gabriel paused. "No, sorry. I meant *absolutely* not."

"Your sense of humor—"

"—is nonexistent. Twelve minutes."

"We haven't started talking."

"You haven't stopped." Gabriel gulped the mocha over his stomach's protests. Then he set down the cup. "I wish to know more about fae compulsion."

"So I'm paying you to ask *me* questions?"

"That's how it works. Questions allow me to refine my investigation. Mr. Lambert claims—"

"Lambert saw a ghost, not a fae."

"Does that mean you can confirm the existence of ghosts?"

"Sure."

"That hardly sounds confident."

"Theoretically, ghosts could exist. I've heard they do. Just never seen one. Liv did, though, right?"

"If you are referring to James, yes, she saw him. Or a vision of him. Or, because she can see visions, she may have been able to see his spirit when others would not. None of that is proof of ghosts. We do, however, have proof of fae."

"It's a ghost, Gabriel. It disappeared. Fae don't disappear."

"Spriggans? Cŵn Annwn?"

"Spriggans can appear to vanish by melding with their surroundings. Camouflage. That only works at a distance. The girl was right in front of Lambert. Cŵn Annwn can trick the eye to, again, *appear* to vanish. But this was a woman. Terribly sexist, our Wild Hunt. The only woman who rides with them is Mallt-y-Nos. Matilda. Which is Liv."

"My point was not that this woman is either spriggan or Huntsman, but that you are incorrect in saying no fae can appear to vanish."

"She isn't fae," Patrick said. "She's a ghost. If you read that research I compiled—"

"Not necessary. I draw my own conclusions based on facts. In this case, I have an eyewitness account."

"As a defense attorney, you should know eye witnesses are notoriously unreliable."

"Only when their testimony does not support my case. In which case, I simply provide experts who will argue the opposite. If you insist on disregarding this particular witness, though, then perhaps the woman *didn't* vanish into thin air after all, which seems to be your primary proof that she's a ghost."

"Huh?" Patrick shook his head. "No wonder you're good at your job. I have no idea what you just said."

"Excellent, then you won't mind humoring me when I say she could be fae, and therefore I need to know more about compulsion. Hypothetically, can a fae plant a subconscious command?"

"A command to do something? We compel you to *not* do things, primarily not to question. Like when you were a boy— I'd talk to you in Cainsville, but when you returned as a young man, you didn't realize I was the same guy you'd spoken to as a child. It's compulsion working in tandem with basic human psychology. It would make no logical sense for me to be the same guy. You decided I must be a relative, which explained the resemblance."

"That's how the Cainsville elders use compulsion. Are you telling me that's the only way it *can* be used?"

"Well, no..."

Gabriel nodded at the next table. "That young woman there. Could you compel her to leave with you?"

"Oh, that doesn't take compulsion."

"Given that she's sitting with another woman, with whom she appears deeply enamored, I wouldn't be so quick to presume that. Let's say she finds you completely unappealing. Could you make her leave with you?"

"No. It's not mind control. If it were, the Cŵn Annwn wouldn't have been working with that CIA shrink."

"Then how about the woman to your right? She *has* been casting her gaze your way. Yet she appears intelligent enough not to walk out of here with a stranger. Could you compel her to leave with you?"

"If I wanted, sure, but I wouldn't. Nor would any self-respecting fae. Now, if I got pulled over by a cop who thought I was cute, would I use compulsion to get out of a ticket? Of course. I'd be crazy not to."

"The key, then, is susceptibility, as it is in all forms of brainwashing. The recipient must be open to it. For Mr. Lambert, one can postulate a basic need to confess. He experienced something inexplicable, and rationally, he knows he shouldn't admit to it, but he wants to. He needs the psychological validation of others, telling him he hasn't lost his mind. Add in picking up a young woman, motivated by something other than paternal concern. He felt guilty and subconsciously compelled to tell his wife."

Patrick rolled his eyes. "Humans. Their warped sense of morality never fails to amaze me."

"There's nothing warped about it. If he is involved in a committed and exclusive relationship, he should not be picking up hitchhikers in hopes of sexual favors. I have little patience with most ethical codes, but that is the violation of a relationship contract rather than a moral one."

"So, by that token, you fear that if you successfully seduced someone who is in a relationship, she would eventually do the same to you. I disagree. You might be the one she wants, and she needs only a sign that you'd reciprocate—"

"Yes, I'm quite certain every man or woman who has seduced someone has told themselves exactly that. She isn't prone to romantic betrayal; he's just special. And while I hope that is another hypothetical, I suspect it is not, and I would tell you to look at the parties involved and realize it would be futile, and even the attempt would be wrong and disrespectful."

"So you admit—"

"We can see, then, that Lambert would be susceptible to fae compulsion."

"She's *not* fae. She's a ghost."

Before Gabriel could answer, his phone rang.

"It's Olivia," he said. "I'll need to take this."

"Just as long as you don't bill me for it."

"Given that she's almost certainly calling in regards to your case, yes, I will. But I will include it as part of your fifteen minutes, which are almost up."

"Generous."

"You haven't seen my bill yet."

Gabriel answered the phone.

"It's me," Olivia said. "My butt needed a break from the bitch seat, so I've been doing research on the case, and I found something you failed to mention. The current circumstances of several of those who met our hitchhiking ghost."

When Gabriel didn't answer, she said, "You haven't dug into the others, have you?"

"I haven't had a chance. I've been focused on Mr. Lambert."

"Ah, this will be fun, then. Where are you?"

He told her.

"Ooh, perfect. Got time for an interview? It'll be quick."

He paused, and she said, "Oh, come on. Humor me." And he couldn't resist that. This sounded like the Olivia he knew, the one he'd driven into hiding.

"All right," he said. "I have a client meeting at two, but I'm free until then."

Patrick cleared his throat. Gabriel said, "One moment," to Olivia and muted the phone before telling Patrick, "I need to follow up on something related to your case," and rising from his seat.

Of course the bòcan protested, but Gabriel made it out of the café before a group of incoming students logjammed the exit.

"I'm heading for my car," he told Olivia. "Presumably, I'll need it."

"Mmm, actually no. Not as long as you're okay walking about a half mile."

"Of course."

"Head east then, and tell me about Lambert."

EIGHT

GABRIEL

GABRIEL WAS deep enough in conversation with Olivia to pay little attention to his surroundings. She directed him, and he walked as they discussed Lambert.

"That *sounds* like fae compulsion," she said, and he caught the emphasis.

"But you have doubts?" he said.

"I'm reserving judgment at the moment. For reasons."

"Which are?"

"Reasons. Unlike our architect friend, I'm not under any compulsion to share thoughts that may make me sound like an idiot. I need more data and your unbiased opinion."

"My opinions are always unbiased."

"Impossible. As soon as people voice an opinion, they're guaranteed to influence our own, depending on our opinion of their competence. And given your opinion of anyone else's competence, I'm keeping my mouth shut."

"I respect your opinions, Olivia."

Silence. He felt it stretch and grow heavy with the weight of the unspoken. The weight of that moment when she'd told him about Gwynn.

"No, Olivia. I'm sorry. You seem to believe this, but it isn't true. In fact, I'm beginning to suspect none of it is true. I understand that you've been in a difficult place, your world turned upside down, and it's easy to get confused—"

"Are you suggesting I'm imagining the visions?"

"Not entirely. I think you've been in a susceptible state, and these creatures—fae, what have you—are taking advantage of that."

"You have a point, though," he said quickly. "The fact that I'm predisposed to trust your opinion would bias me in favor of your conclusion. So you don't think this is fae, then? Patrick insists we're dealing with a ghost."

"Have you reached the mausoleum yet?"

"Maus…" He trailed off as he looked around to realize he was not cutting through a park, but a cemetery. He glanced over his shoulder. "I see one about fifty feet back. It appears to be the only structure on this particular path."

"You walk too fast. You know that?" Forced lightness in her voice. "Okay, back up and make a right—no, that'd be a left now—at the mausoleum."

She continued to direct him. When she told him to stop, he knew what he'd see. He said nothing, though, letting her play this out.

"Okay, turn left," she said. "Take three steps."

"If I take three, I'll ruin my loafer and possibly break my toes bashing into a headstone."

"Three normal-person steps, Gabriel. Headstone. Read it."

"Generous of heart, constant of faith—"

"Blah, blah, blah," she said, and he had to smile at that. "Read the important part."

"One could argue that the inscription left by the family *is* the important—"

"Yeah, yeah. You're just playing with me now."

"Tanya Elizabeth Gross," he said. "She's one of those who reported seeing the woman in white."

"Got your notes handy?"

"Of course." He pulled them up on his phone as Olivia said, "Check the date."

Tanya Gross had died two days after she reported picking up the woman in white.

Forty-eight hours.

He opened his mouth to tell Olivia that. Then he stopped. She wasn't the only one who feared looking foolish by jumping to conclusions.

"And the others?" he said. "You mentioned *several*."

"Slight exaggeration. Seven people have reported seeing the woman in white over the past couple of years. Two are dead. Both died two days later. I'm sending you the obits. Tell me if you see another commonality."

He opened the clippings and skimmed them. "Suicide." Not that either obituary said that outright, but he recognized the language. "Died suddenly" for Tanya Gross and "Unexpected passing" for Blair Cohen.

"Yep. I've confirmed that. Tanya took a swan dive off an office building, and Blair put a gun to his temple."

"Both forty-eight hours after they reported seeing the woman in white."

He told her about Lambert's frenzied vacation planning. Which he apparently had forty-eight hours to do.

"Yeah," she said. "That wasn't a sale. He was rationalizing a compulsion."

"It would seem so, but compelled to plan a trip? That seems odd."

"The trip is the solution to a problem. His wife is pissed off. He's trying to placate her."

"To undo the damage *caused* by the report he was *compelled* to make? That seems labyrinthine."

"Yeah, I'm lost, too."

Lost.

That chill prickled down his neck.

A moment passed. Then, "Gabriel? You still there?"

"Of course."

"There's something else you should see. Turn right."

"If it's Cohen's grave, I don't think that's necessary."

"He's not buried here. It's… No, you're right. It isn't necessary, and you're supposed to be working. I'll just send you—"

"I don't have to leave for another thirty minutes. Turn right, you said?"

A pause, and Gabriel could sense he was losing her.

A little late for that.

He pushed aside Gwynn's voice. What Gabriel meant was Olivia's good mood was fading, as something must have reminded her that they weren't where they'd been. That things had changed.

"I'm walking right," he said. "I'm almost back at the main path."

Silence.

"Olivia?"

He heard her inhale, and he braced for her to find an excuse and cut the call short.

Tell her about the memory. The woman in the abandoned building.

No. Sharing something like that opened him up to pity. Sympathy. A reminder of the boy he'd been, the part of his life he wished Olivia didn't know. He preferred to have materialized whole cloth in his present form. Arrogant. Self-centered. Insensitive. No excuses. That felt better. Felt safer.

"Look, you're busy," she said. "And I'm just goofing around, killing time while Ricky talks shop with Don. I shouldn't make you entertain me."

"You aren't."

Uncomfortable silence because that was just an excuse, taking blame on herself rather than putting it where it belonged.

I don't want to do this, Gabriel. It's not safe.

"I remembered something that might—" he began, but she was talking at the same time, saying, "Are you back at the mausoleum yet?"

"I just passed it."

Another laugh, strained now. "Of course you did. Go back there and turn left."

She continued with her directions, leading him into an older part of the cemetery. When she told him to stop, he stood in front of an elaborate tombstone, with an angel perched on top.

"Christina Anne Moore," he read, without being prompted, and then the dates: 1947–1967.

"If this is one of the early victims, she'd have been one of the very first," he said. "My research had the first report of the hitchhiking ghost in the late sixties."

"Nineteen sixty-eight," Olivia said. "I'm sending you an article now."

She did, and he opened it to see a photograph of a young woman with long blond hair. The headline read "Roadside Tragedy Claims Young Cellist."

Gabriel skimmed the article. In 1967, twenty-year-old Christina Moore had been hitchhiking home from Chicago after attending a music festival. She'd been dropped off along a regional highway. As she walked, both night and a summer shower fell, visibility falling with them. A pickup truck veering onto the shoulder had struck Christina Moore with enough force to send her flying twenty feet into a field.

"She wasn't found for days," Olivia said. "The guy said he thought he hit a deer. A deer wearing a white sundress, apparently. But that aside, does it sound familiar?"

"It does."

"So, good reason to think she's not fae?"

"Yes, it appears Patrick was right. We have a ghost."

NINE

PATRICK

GABRIEL WAS in a cemetery. Could it get any more perfect than that? Patrick only regretted that he hadn't foreseen this in time to prep the scene. But it would have been impossible to foresee it... when he still wasn't sure what Gabriel was doing here.

As Patrick followed Gabriel—at a proper distance, of course—he tried to figure out what Liv was up to. That was still Liv on the phone. Patrick could tell, not only by the length of the call but by his son's very gait, no longer chewing up sidewalks as if they were obstacles separating him from a goal. He was practically strolling, purposeful stride slowed to a brisk walk, his shoulders relaxed, cell phone at his ear.

As they'd left the rush of the streets, Patrick worried he'd be spotted, so he'd circled around, presuming Gabriel was just cutting through the cemetery. He wasn't. Patrick lost him then, and he'd been wandering when he'd caught the rumble of his son's deep voice.

Patrick arrived just in time to see Gabriel on the move again, heading out from a row of tombstones, looking less relaxed now, almost anxious. One might think he'd seen something in the grave-yard that upset him, but only Liv could cause that particular look, the one that reminded Patrick of a man hanging from a cliff, thinking he'd found a good handhold and then feeling the edge crumble under his fingers.

Patrick circled around and tried to figure out which gravestone Gabriel had been looking at, but Gabriel's worry seemed to pulse through the air, shattering his concentration. Which was vexing. It wasn't as if Patrick had never had a son before. He'd left enough children in his wake to populate a small city.

He could say Gabriel was different because Gabriel was Gwynn, and with Matilda, they represented Cainsville's best hope of survival. Patrick admittedly wasn't eager to abandon the town. He'd made a place for himself there. A home. He might affect the glamour of a young man, but in fae terms, he was entering his twilight years and, like humans of that life stage, he could not overestimate the appeal of a home, a safe place to rest both body and mind. At the thought of finding a new refuge, his entire being screeched, "I'm too old for this shit."

Yet it was more than that. More than worry that Gwynn wouldn't win his Matilda, and Cainsville would crumble. Gwynn didn't *need* to win Matilda. Cainsville and the Tylwyth Teg needed to convince her to choose them over the Cŵn Annwn. Having Gwynn for her lover only helped cement her ties to their side.

So why fret about Gabriel and his relationship with Liv? Because Liv made Gabriel happy, and Patrick wanted his son to be happy. A simple thing for a human father. For fae? Nearly unfathomable. They sired children to spread their blood, infiltrating the ranks, so to speak. Like human populations dealing with invaders. Survival by biological assimilation.

So it had been with the scores of children Patrick sired. But with Gabriel, Patrick couldn't just sow his seed and waltz off. Gabriel was Gwynn. Gabriel had to be kept close and nurtured.

Which Patrick had completely and utterly failed at.

It wasn't even guilt that drew him to his son now. Not entirely. There was more, but he wouldn't waste time on self-analysis. Leave psychotherapy to humans. It was enough for Patrick to acknowledge there was more.

Now, where *was* his son? Patrick had been following him, and then Gabriel had walked behind a mausoleum and, *poof,* vanished like a ghost. Which was impossible. First, Patrick wasn't certain there were such things as ghosts. Second, Gabriel didn't *vanish* even in a crowd. So where had—?

Patrick spotted him. Gabriel had veered off course and stood in front of yet another gravestone, cell phone still at his ear. He was relaxed now, that tightness gone from his profile. He'd recaptured Liv. Well, recaptured her attention, which was step one.

While Gabriel was stationary and distracted, Patrick had a chance to stage his story. To bring a ghost to life. He just had to figure out how to do that. So...

Gabriel is in a cemetery. A cemetery. *The stage is prepped and waiting. You're a writer. Here's your setting. Give me a scene.*

The harder he thought, though, the more his muse whined about the unsatisfactory conditions. It was broad daylight. There were people milling about. Gabriel wasn't near anything Patrick could hide behind.

Honestly, what was he supposed to do? Sneak up behind him and make ghost noises?

Patrick needed time. He needed props. He needed a cloudy night and a bitter wind whispering through treetops.

And now Gabriel was on the move again. Of course he was, damn him. Patrick set out at a jog, watching and assessing. When he realized Gabriel was heading out of the cemetery, Patrick let out a curse. Then he saw that his son's trajectory put him in line with the mausoleum.

Yes!

Patrick raced behind the building and shed his glamour. First, of course, he made sure no one was watching, his natural form being somewhat more…noticeable than other fae's.

Glamour gone, he pressed against the ivy-covered side of the mausoleum. Then he reached up. In fae form, he was taller than his human self, with longer and thinner limbs. He leaped and caught the edge of the roof. Then he scuttled onto it and pressed down again, letting himself meld with the vines and moss as he wriggled across to the far side. He got there just as Gabriel started passing underneath.

Patrick made ghost noises. Well, what a real ghost *might* sound like, sibilant whispers rather than the moaning and clamoring of the fictional variety. His son slowed. Then he stopped directly under the roofline.

Patrick leaned out as far as he dared and added words to his whispers. Key words, like "help" and "please."

Gabriel stayed still. Listening intently.

"Help," Patrick whispered. "Please. I need—"

"Yes, that's an excellent idea," Gabriel said into the phone. "I'll do that right now." He resumed walking and shifted his cell to his other ear. "That's fine. Have a safe trip. Give me a call when you stop for the night, and I'll let you know what I've found."

Patrick growled, startling a squirrel peeking over the roofline. The beast saw him and shrieked and tore off. Patrick retreated across the roof, dropped to the ground and snapped his glamour back in place. As he did, he caught a movement to his left and spun fast, peering down the row of headstones.

He had surveyed the scene before climbing down. It'd been clear. But now he was sure he'd spotted a figure amongst the tombstones.

And, yes, that sounded exactly like the sort of thing he'd tried to conjure up for Gabriel. Which suggested his mind was playing a nasty and mocking trick.

Patrick was about to turn away when he caught the flicker again. He turned and...

And there was a woman standing by a grave. The same tomb Gabriel had visited.

Patrick hesitated. He even blinked a few times, as if a ray of sunshine might be manifesting in human shape, because that was a far more believable explanation than this—that there was a woman where there had been no one only moments ago.

Not just a woman, either, but a blonde in a white sundress.

No, he was seeing things. His imagination having fun with him.

The woman bent and touched her fingers to the gravestone. Patrick made his way toward her as silently as he could, loosening his glamour, his natural form better suited for sneaking across a green lawn.

He drew close enough to see the woman clearly. To make out her face. Her form. She was young, with straight blond hair and wore a sundress fifty years out of date. Her feet were bare, and she reminded him of the girls he'd toy with back when her sundress was fashionable—girls who'd found his looks particularly appealing, that whiff of the fae even in his glamour. He'd played that to full effect. The girls themselves had reminded *him* of some fae, ethereal, flighty and not-quite-there will-o'-the-wisps.

That alone drew him closer, even as he warned himself. When he focused his vision, he caught a telltale shimmer. It seemed not a fae's glow but a smudge to the young woman's edges. A feathering. A blurring.

He took one more step...and a twig cracked under his foot. She spun and stared at him.

Then she disappeared.

TEN

GABRIEL

GABRIEL WALKED into Lambert's office, where the architect was shredding papers, the sound loud enough to cover Gabriel's entry. He slowed and approached offside to see what Lambert was shredding. While people had very good reasons for destroying papers, to a defense lawyer, it was always suspicious. But Lambert wasn't destroying anything. He appeared to be pushing blank pages into the machine, feeding them through one at a time, his gaze fixed out the window.

"I don't believe those require shredding," Gabriel said.

The architect gave a start. He stared, as if trying to place Gabriel, despite the fact he'd been there only hours before. And Gabriel had been told he was rather memorable.

"Those pages," Gabriel said. "Unless they're written in invisible ink, I don't believe they need to be destroyed."

Lambert turned the sheaf of papers over in his hand, giving them that same uncomprehending stare.

"I was…I need to…"

"Get back on track," Gabriel said.

"Yes."

"Because you're lost."

Lambert blinked. "What?"

"Never mind. I need you to do something for me." He took printed pages from his pocket. "I would like you to look at several photographs and tell me if you recognize anyone in connection with your encounter."

"Encounter…"

"With the hitchhiking young woman."

Lambert recoiled as if Gabriel had poked him with a cattle prod.

"I don't know her," Lambert said. "I'd never met her before, and I don't want anything to do with her. It was all a mistake. I love my wife. She's a wonderful—"

"Yes, yes, I'm sure she is. But as I may have said before, I am working to corroborate your story. I want to see justice done."

Meaningless babble, but it was enough—a reassurance that someone was on Lambert's side.

Gabriel unfolded the sheets. At Olivia's suggestion, he'd created a makeshift police lineup. He'd done this sort of thing with witnesses before, using websites where he could submit a scanned photo and search for similar ones. He'd chosen three and done some fiddling with Christina Moore's photograph so it wasn't as obviously out of date. Now he laid the four pictures in front of Lambert.

"Do any of these women look familiar?"

It took two sweeps. The first held that blank-eyed expression, Lambert still unfocused. But then he pulled himself together enough to do a proper scan, and his finger landed on the photograph of Christina Moore.

"That's her. That's the girl I picked up." Lambert flushed. "As a hitchhiker, I mean."

"Understood. Thank you for your time."

Gabriel turned to go. He made it three steps. Then he caught sight of a clock on the wall.

Forty-eight hours.

He thought of Tanya Gross, the first gravestone he'd visited.

He heard Lambert again, frantically trying to book that vacation, the deadline looming.

Gabriel turned back to the architect, who was poised behind his desk, as if they were still mid-conversation.

"Mr. Lambert," he said.

"Yes?"

"In the course of my investigation, I've had contact with your wife. I say this in complete confidence, because I doubt she would want me sharing it, but I believe it's important for you to know."

"Yes?"

"She forgives you. She will not say that immediately, perhaps not for a while, and you must continue to work at repairing the damage, but your eagerness to repair it has been recognized."

Lambert stood there, as if waiting for something Gabriel's words did not quite provide. Which was rather annoying. It seemed clear enough, and to say more made him feel like he was auditioning for a post as Rose's assistant.

Gabriel steeled himself. "You've found the right path. You're back on it." A moment's pause, and then he added, "Stay on it," before leaving.

⤜⤏

SO they appeared to have a ghost. Which did not bother Gabriel nearly as much as an illogical construct within the expected narrative.

Christina Moore died on a lonely stretch of road, hit by a careless driver on a rainy summer night. For fifty years since that night, witnesses had reported picking up a hitchhiking ghost matching Christina's description, all within that general region, all on rainy nights.

To this point, the narrative made logical sense. If ghosts existed, might they not be souls trapped on earth, trying to complete one final task? Endlessly and fruitlessly trying, in Christina's case.

Here was where the logic broke down. For the first forty-odd years, when someone stopped to pick up her ghost, she could not tell them where she wished to go. She would break down in tears...and then disappear.

Then, in the last two years, the narrative had changed, as if Christina suddenly remembered where she needed to be. But then she started giving *false* directions designed to lead drivers off the road. To get them lost. Whereupon she'd impart a final message before vanishing. And forty-eight hours later, at least two who had picked her up killed themselves.

So what had changed?

Gabriel pondered this question as he sat across from a client in the Cook County Jail. Ostensibly, he was listening to Mr. Pryce, but that required only the occasional nod or murmur. Had Pryce been talking about his own case, he would deserve all Gabriel's focus, but he was simply bemoaning the fact he might spend the next ten years in jail.

Gabriel could point out that he had every hope of getting the sentence down to three years, possibly four, but he had learned that it was not the length of time that clients found daunting. It was the "in jail" part. And while Gabriel knew enough to listen and nod and make those noises that could be interpreted as sympathy, it was all he could do not to give an exasperated, "What did you expect?"

It was truly astounding how the human mind worked. People committed crimes—in this case, hiring a hitman to kill a business partner—and then whined about the punishment once they were caught. Even as a child, Gabriel had known the potential consequences of his youthful criminality. It had begun right with Seanna when she'd made a game of teaching him to pickpocket money from her men. If he won, he shared in the profits, via a candy bar or a trip to the used bookstore. If he was caught, though? That was on him, and Gabriel better not even *try* implicating Seanna.

When he was eight, his mother sent him on his first break-and-enter. He was to sneak into the home of one of her lovers and fetch back the money the man had allegedly stolen from her—which Gabriel presumed was money she'd paid him for drugs. While he was inside, he was free to take anything else he found, and they'd split the profits, fifty-fifty, in cash. That led to his first mistake—and his first lesson in the perils of greed. He'd been so fixated on the monetary reward that he'd stayed too long, and the man's wife had returned, glimpsing him as he dove out the window.

Seanna said if the police came, she'd turn him over, and he'd be in prison until his twentieth birthday. Even as a child, this struck Gabriel as rather extreme, and so he'd done what he always did when Seanna told him something he suspected was untrue: he looked it up. And there he got his first taste of the law, like the Theban labyrinth with the Minotaur at the center, surrounded by endless traps and hidden escape routes.

That Minotaur? Jail time. It could be avoided, yet once you stepped into the maze—once you committed a crime—you accepted the possibility that prison might be your fate. Or, in the words of the cliché, if you can't do the time, don't do the crime.

Gabriel had always kept that in mind, always known that if he did something and was caught, he'd pay the price. After turning eighteen, he had—largely—given up pickpocketing and burglary and other acts likely to end in a prison cell. But if he did commit them, and he was caught, while he'd try his best to avoid the Minotaur, he would never whine and moan like his clients. Seanna had taught him correctly in that: take responsibility for your actions.

She'd also inadvertently taught him to commit his own crimes and not pay others to do them for you. Which made this client's wailing all the more annoying. Gabriel had to stop accepting clients who hired hitmen. He simply could not work up the proper degree of patience with them.

"You know what's really not fair?" Pryce said.

Life, Gabriel was tempted to answer, which, while true, no one ever wanted to hear. So he made his noise, one that could be mistaken for a "Hmm?" of actual interest.

"I didn't *kill* anyone. No one's claiming I did. But I'm still going to prison. How exactly can Lou's death be *my* fault?"

Possibly because you paid the person who *did* pull the trigger? Paid him *to* pull it?

"It's not my fault," Pryce said. "Not at all."

And with those words, Gabriel finally saw the problem. Not with Pryce, who had too many problems to note, but with the ghost of Christina Moore.

"Culpability," he murmured.

The client's face screwed up. "What?"

"You feel you were not responsible," Gabriel said, as if by rote. That's what they wanted to hear. Well, no. They wanted to hear "You are not responsible," but even Gabriel had limits to what he could say with a straight face.

"Damn right I'm not responsible. I don't understand how I'm even being charged with this. Like I said, I didn't actually want this guy to kill Lou. It was… What do you call it? Entrapment. I thought he was kidding. And if he says otherwise, well, he's a killer. He lies. Look at me. I'm an educated, successful businessman. A pillar of my community. You're going to tell the jury that, right? Pillar of my community?"

Gabriel made another noncommittal noise. Those were four words he would never utter in front of a judge. It might as well be shorthand for "My client sponsored a little league baseball team to hide the fact he's a murdering scumbag."

As his client continued, Gabriel mentally reversed to the concept of culpability. That was what bothered him about the ghost case. What did her victims do to deserve an apparent death curse? A man who considered cheating on his wife was in need of either a wakeup call or a divorce lawyer. But death? That was like punishing a first-time pickpocket with double amputation.

Moreover, Lambert's case *did* smack of entrapment—offering an enticing possibility and seeing if Lambert would take the bait. And it had absolutely nothing to do with Christina Moore's fate. Yes, a ghost's revenge could be unconnected to her death, but why change her modus operandi from panicked tears to cold-blooded murder? Was there an inciting event? Or some missed connection between her death and her curses?

His client was still expostulating on the terrible unfairness of his situation. Gabriel was still pretending to listen. When he caught a break in the rant, he murmured, "Yes," accompanied by a solemn nod, and received a grunt of satisfaction in reply.

Your outrage has been noted. In billable hours.

"You are going to get me out of here, right?"

Eventually.

"As I've said, Mr. Pryce, the charges against you, while"—*fair*—"reprehensible, are grave, and since, under psychological duress, you made the"—*idiotic*—"understandable mistake of confessing to hiring"—*some lowlife thug who kills for beer money*—"a professional assassin, the task of setting you free is contingent upon"—*divine intervention*—"an exceedingly favorable jury, which we are unlikely to get in light of that confession. Our hope is that the jury will"—*be equally idiotic and possibly sociopathic*—"see the unfairness of your situation and reduce your sentence accordingly."

Count on four years. Possibly three, if I decide you're worth the extra effort.

Pryce stared at Gabriel, running on a thirty-second delay as he struggled to process all that. After a few moments, he nodded and said, "I get it. Sure. Thanks."

"Be assured, I'm doing my best." *Or a reasonable facsimile of it.*

GABRIEL strode to his car and took his phone from the locked glove compartment. Earlier he'd e-mailed Olivia the results of Lambert's photo lineup, and now she'd just gotten back to him with: *Okay, so we have a ghost. If I say that's cool, you won't roll your eyes at me, right?*

Never.

And if you do, I'm not there to see it, so I can pretend it never happened :) Give me a shout if you get a minute. We'll be back on the road soon. Almost home!

He checked the time stamp against the clock. She'd sent it ten minutes ago. He called her. It rang three times. Then a male voice answered with, "Hey, Gabriel."

"Ricky..."

"Yeah, Liv ran to the restroom. I was going to ignore the call. Then I saw it was you. So, ghost, huh? That's cool."

There was no sarcasm in his voice. Gabriel wished there were— that little twist that said Ricky couldn't believe Liv found this interesting. Perhaps the eye-roll she'd expected from Gabriel. But Gabriel didn't need to see Ricky's face to know the sentiment was genuine. As was the rest—answering the phone to be sure Liv got his message, never thinking to click the Ignore button, perhaps finding a way to hide any trace of the call. In other words, never considering everything Gabriel would if the situation were reversed.

Because Ricky was "a nice guy." A decent guy. A good person. Pick your platitude. All those hackneyed phrases that should make Gabriel curl his lip and dismiss Ricky with contempt and disgust. Nice. Good. Decent. Synonyms for weak, foolish and ineffectual. Unless you were Ricky.

Ricky Gallagher was a biker. And an MBA student. At least one of those things should make him an asshole. The combination should make him an insufferable lout.

But Ricky Gallagher was not an ass. Or insufferable. Or weak, foolish or ineffectual. He rose above all that, naturally, to be tough and smart as well as likable and charming.

Worse, Gabriel could not even muster a good dose of jealous hatred. Which had not stopped him from watching Ricky dangle, injured, from a bell tower and thinking how easy it would be to let him fall. It had, however, stopped Gabriel from doing so. And left him reflecting on that dark impulse with the most uncomfortable of emotions: shame.

"Gabriel?"

"Yes. We have a case. I was phoning with an update, but it isn't urgent. Olivia can call me in the morning."

"Whoa, no. If I let you go, I'll catch proper shit. You've got her hooked with the mystery. I'm keeping you on the line, like it or not."

A chuckle, a little bit forced, a reminder that Olivia wasn't the only one Gabriel had hurt. Not the only one he'd betrayed. And Ricky didn't even know about his hesitation in the bell tower.

Fresh shame licked through Gabriel.

Ricky continued, "And because I know you despise small talk, my dad wants me to run a few things past you when I get back. Normal business." Which meant the Gallaghers' legitimate business interests, rather than their criminal ones. "He wants me to handle it, but if you'd rather—"

"No, that's fine. We'll talk."

"Great. And here comes Liv." Ricky's voice faded, as if pulling the phone away. "It's Gabriel. I told him you're not interested in the case, and you don't want to hear anything about it."

Whatever Olivia did, it made Ricky laugh. Then he said into the receiver. "Here she is. I'll call Lydia tomorrow and set up a meeting."

Olivia came on the line with a breezy, "Hey, there." Gabriel eased back in the driver's seat and told her what was bothering him about Christina Moore.

"Exactly what I was thinking," Olivia said. "It's a one-eighty in haunting style. Weepy ghost to vengeful spirit with no apparent transition period. I say 'apparent' meaning I have to dig deeper to confirm that. To that end, I've tracked down the woman who claims to have encountered weepy Chrissy right before Tanya Gross—the first to fall to the vengeful version."

"Excellent. We can speak to her tomorrow."

"Actually, I thought Ricky and I would pop by there tonight."

A chill settled between Gabriel's shoulder blades. A dangerous chill. The one that slid into his gut and made his voice ice over as he said, "I see."

Olivia did not fail to catch that chill. She hurried on, saying, "She lives outside the city. Right on our way to Cainsville. It makes sense for us to stop by."

"Of course."

He heard his chill deepen, and he tried to put on the brakes, change direction, avoid this destination. She was right. It was efficient. No insult to him. No rejection. So why did he feel that same impulse rising? To reject. To shun. To freeze her out. Just as he had when she'd told him about Gwynn.

"Unless you'd rather I waited," she said. "Or maybe you want to do it yourself?"

"No, of course not. Your plan makes sense."

A wary, "Okay," as if she suspected it wasn't *okay* at all. "So we'll pop by, and then I'll call you with whatever I learn—"

"No," he said. "I'll be busy tonight." Stop. Damn it. *Stop. Reverse.* "I'm very busy, Olivia. I'm still catching up from before, and I really don't have time for this case."

"Okay…" *Uh, weren't you the one who suggested it, Gabriel?* She didn't say that. She would have, a few weeks ago. Now she trod carefully. So carefully.

Back up. Tell her you were joking. She'll laugh and say you need a lot more practice, and you'll insist it's fine for her to conduct that interview with Ricky. Just call when she's done and—

"If you wish to pursue it, you may do so," he said. "I'll let Patrick know. But I don't have the time. Now, if you'll excuse me, I need to get back to work."

ELEVEN

GABRIEL

GABRIEL WAS in the gym. He'd been there often enough in the last two weeks for the staff to notice and say it was good to see him coming regularly. One made the mistake of clapping Gabriel on the shoulder. One glance, and the man had pulled away so fast you'd think he'd been in imminent danger of losing the limb. Today, as Gabriel stalked in, the young woman behind the desk hadn't even waited to see his membership card, just pointed mutely at the locker rooms.

He had excuses for increasing the regularity of his visits. With Olivia away, he had more time. And he may, in hauling Ricky onto that balcony, have realized how long it'd been since he'd done more than go for a run or a swim.

There was also the undeniable fact that his physique did not fare well under poor diet and exercise conditions. A large bone structure meant it was easy for him to gain muscle...and equally easy to gain not-muscle. Also easy for him to conceal the not-muscle. Or conceal it until he shed his shirt and proved it had been a while since he could feign a flat stomach without inhaling.

Any impetus, then, to rectify the problem came from a personal desire to get back into shape. Fix the problem before he reached middle age and a soft middle became a spare tire. It had absolutely nothing to do with the fact that Ricky was in excellent shape and in possession of not only a flat stomach but the proverbial six-pack.

That was not what drove him to the gym.

At least it wasn't tonight, because tonight, the very thought of considering how his physique compared to Ricky's was laughable. Rather like worrying that his swimming skills weren't on par with an Olympian's. It wasn't as if he had any chance of joining an Olympic swim team…and at this moment, possibly more chance of that than ever having Olivia see him with his shirt off. He seemed hell-bent on making sure of *that*.

Which was why he was here tonight—trying to work off the anger and the frustration. If he couldn't focus enough to lose himself in work, he would work himself into physical exhaustion and then perhaps…

Perhaps what? Reach some mental nirvana of clarity? Understand why he seemed determined to sabotage *any* relationship with Olivia?

It was one thing to not understand what he was doing wrong. In the beginning, he'd had that excuse. When he'd betrayed her, he'd honestly felt—okay, *mostly* felt—that he'd done nothing wrong. He knew better now, having gained a sufficient grasp of what it meant to hold a person's trust. To betray that trust. To hurt that person.

And yet now he saw the problem…and couldn't stop making it worse. Like watching a freight train barreling downhill and holding up his hands, shouting, "Stop!" only to have it roll right over him.

Olivia wanted to conduct one interview with Ricky, for a very good reason, and the logical part of his brain knew it had nothing to do with him. But it felt like rejection, and his defenses had shot into place.

You won't hurt me.

I won't let you.

I'll hurt you first.

He hefted the barbell over his chest, too much weight, his muscles screaming. He kept lifting, pushing higher and—

His cell phone sounded with a text message. He struggled to get the barbell into the rack and pulled out his phone.

It was Olivia.

Made it to Cainsville. Can come in tomorrow if helps with workload.

Gabriel squeezed his eyes shut and leaned against the machine, feeling as if he still held that barbell, muscles trembling, weight threatening to crush him. He mentally repeated the text and heard the hesitation, so very un-Olivia.

Treading carefully. Walking on eggshells around his mood because she had to. Because he was her boss, and she loved her job, and it was his to take away. Because he had, subtly, threatened that before.

Which was not how a friendship was supposed to work.

Not at all.

You're clearly upset, Gabriel, and I'm afraid of losing my job, so I'll come back early to help out.

He started typing a response.

No, that's fine.

Too curt. She'd think he was angry.

No, you don't need to.

Too ambiguous. She might think he was testing her. Or worse, that he was saying he didn't need her at work. Ever.

Stay home. Rest up! You'll need it after that long ride. See you Monday!

Oh, yes. That was perfect…if he wanted her to think he'd been drugged. Possibly possessed.

There was no message he could send that she wouldn't spend far too much time analyzing. He needed to fix this in person. Immediately. Before he lost his nerve.

GABRIEL had lost his nerve.

It started partway through the drive when he began worrying that it would seem odd if he drove out to Cainsville just to talk to Olivia. It would look as if their friendship was important to him, and he worried that he'd lost it. Which was clearly true, but the thought of showing up on her doorstep and proving—

No, he needed an excuse.

He would go to Rose's. His great-aunt lived right across the road from Olivia's apartment. He'd stop in for a visit and then, while he was in the neighborhood, he really ought to speak to Olivia and make sure she didn't feel obligated to come to work. And if that led to talk of the ghost, he could say that he had spoken in haste, momentarily feeling overwhelmed by work, and he *did* have time to pursue it, if she was so inclined.

That's when he drove onto Rowan and saw Ricky's motorcycle parked in front of Olivia's building.

He almost turned around right then. Circled the block and headed home. But two of the elders had waved to him on Main Street. How would he explain that if they mentioned it to Olivia?

So he parked and walked to Rose's door. He'd just rung the bell when a laugh floated out from her open front window. Olivia's laugh.

Gabriel glanced at his car.

Yes, excellent plan. Run quickly, and perhaps they'll only see your taillights as you speed away.

The door opened.

"Ricky," Gabriel said.

"Hey." Ricky stepped back. "Good timing. Your aunt was just making tea."

"I didn't realize you and Olivia were here. I should have called. Tell Rose I'll speak to her tomorrow."

"She's right here. Come on in. Liv will want to say hi."

No, Gabriel was quite certain Olivia did not want to say hello. Not to him. Which Ricky would know, having been party to their last conversation. He was trying to broker peace, as he always did. Trying to do the right thing, as he always did.

I thought of letting you fall off that balcony.

I thought of letting you die.

Gabriel's gut clenched, and he was about to make his apologies when Olivia swung in with her usual grin, her green eyes dancing. Then she saw who was at the door.

That light snuffed out. A moment's pause before she fixed on a smile that made his gut clench all the more. The gracious debutante smile she used for strangers.

"Hello," she said. Not "Hey." Not "Hi." Not some teasing comment about him appearing just in time for cookies.

"I was just—" Gabriel began.

"I should take off," Ricky said. "I can still make it back to the city before dark, and Dad was hoping to talk to me tonight."

"And I have"—Olivia visibly struggled—"laundry."

"I think it can wait," Ricky said. "As bad as it smells, another day can't possibly make it any worse."

"Ha-ha. Yes, I'm making a crappy excuse." She turned to Gabriel. "You want to talk to Rose, so I'll clear out."

"No, I—"

"It's fine. We were just chatting. I'll see you at work tomorrow?"

"That won't be necessary."

He meant it in the most thoughtful and considerate way, but his voice was not accustomed to displaying either tone. Olivia tensed, and Ricky's jaw set in a look that warned Gabriel he was one step from seeing a far less pleasant side of the young biker.

Gabriel hurried on, "You've had a long trip, and you weren't due back in the office until Monday, so you should take the extra day and rest."

Do laundry. That's what he would have added a few weeks ago, with a quirk of his lips, and she'd have laughed. Now he could no more manage it than she could manage her usual grin.

But what he did say seemed enough, Ricky giving a slight nod and easing back, Olivia relaxing and saying, "No, I'll be in. I'd rather get up to speed and ready for Monday."

"All right, then. As for the ghost—"

"No ghost stories. Got it. And I'm sorry if I got carried away. You were humoring Patrick, but this isn't a real case. My undivided attention will be on that: real cases."

Before he could say anything more, she hurried out the door with Ricky. Gabriel stood there, watching them go. As he shut the door, footsteps sounded behind him.

"May I ask you a favor, Gabriel?"

He turned. His aunt's expression was unreadable, which meant she was about to say something that would upset him, and so she tread carefully. He'd left once before, not to return for years, and while that had been about protecting her, it had still hurt, a fact he only realized in retrospect. To Rose, it had felt like rejection, and so, as solid as their relationship might be now, she tread as lightly as Olivia. It was like the punch line to a poor joke. How do you have a

relationship with someone who can't fully grasp the concept? Very, very carefully.

Rose walked closer. "It's about Liv."

He took shallow breaths. If he stiffened, she'd back off, and whatever she had to say, he needed to hear it.

"If you're having second thoughts about her job—" Rose began.

He tried to protest, but she held up her hand and continued. "If you are, I'm going to ask that you tough it out for six months, and then you help her find a new position and offer a glowing recommendation. She deserves that."

"I'm not—"

"She gave up her job at the diner to work for you. Yes, that wasn't exactly a sacrifice. She has a graduate degree. She shouldn't be waiting tables. But nor, one could argue, should she be a private investigator. You offered her the job, and she loves it, and no one else is going to hire her until she has more experience."

"Yes, of course. I—"

"Liv doesn't even need to work, but she wants to. And she wants the job you gave her. She's been a damned fine investigator."

"I know. I—"

"So do not let your personal issues threaten that, Gabriel. She doesn't deserve it. Those issues? I'm sorry—you know I hate to say this—but they are yours. Exclusively yours."

He pulled back, and he heard her sigh softly. He steadied himself and said, "I have no intention of firing Olivia. I do not employ her out of charity. She does her job very well, and thus there would be no legal grounds to dismiss her."

"We aren't talking about legal grounds, Gabriel."

"I know. What I'm trying to say is that if she thinks her job is in danger, I will set her straight on that point. We had a personal dispute. I told her not to come into work. I only meant for one day—I was upset. But even that crossed a line. Her job is secure, and if I've made her feel otherwise, I will rectify the misunderstanding."

"Good. Now come inside."

"I should—"

"Does that sentence end with the words 'go and speak to Olivia'?"

He said nothing.

"Then come inside," she said as she headed for the kitchen. "Someone needs to drink this tea now that you've frightened off my guests."

Gabriel followed her. "That was not my intention. I was simply coming to speak to you about…" He thought fast. "Ghosts. I want to speak to you about ghosts."

She glanced over her shoulder. "For this case that you told Liv you don't have time to investigate…after dangling it in front of her like a lollipop."

He cleared his throat. "That too is a misunderstanding. I only meant that she should not feel obligated to pursue this whim of Patrick's when she has just returned from vacation."

"Excellent excuse. Stick to it. Now go sit in the parlor."

He did. As he sat in front of Rose's desk, he saw a new book on top. *Discovering Cape Breton Folklore*. A gift from Olivia. He was leafing through it when Rose came in with the tea tray. He put the book aside and rose to pour tea, then took a cookie as he sat.

"First," she said, "before we talk ghosts, tell me you aren't wasting my time."

He arched his brows.

"You know what I mean, Gabriel. Tell me you aren't going to pick my brain and then chicken out on pursuing the case."

"Chicken out? That's rather colorful."

"Rather accurate, too, but fine, let me reword that. Tell me you won't waste my time by deciding tomorrow that you are far, far too busy to pursue this case."

"Olivia may not wish to—"

"Then you will. You'll give her that excuse about not wanting to waste her time. You'll tell her you are still pursuing it and that you would appreciate her help—as paid employment. So yes?"

He made a noise.

"Try again, Gabriel. Yes, Rose, I promise I am not wasting your time. I'm asking Olivia to come ghost hunting with me."

"I would hardly call it—"

"Yes?"

"Yes. To…what you said."

"Good. Ask your questions."

TWELVE

GABRIEL

GABRIEL RARELY regretted his rhetorical style. It was not showy or flashy, and on seeing a lawyer stage the courtroom equivalent of a melodrama, while he could appreciate the effectiveness, it did not appeal to him. He watched lawyers gesture and mug and cast the defendant in the role of saint—or misbegotten sinner—and he felt a moue of distaste. That was showmanship, not skill. Like a pickpocket who shouts, "Fire!" in a crowded room because he's not good enough to empty a pocket with light fingers and a nudge of misdirection.

Gabriel did his best work outside the courtroom. Building the case. Gathering the evidence. Arranging it to fit his narrative and, yes, sometimes filling in the holes with carefully constructed fictions. In the courtroom, while he certainly employed some legal sleight of hand and misdirection, his defense seemed simple and straightforward, and it was given in the same tone. Direct. Economical. Confident. No flourishes or digressions.

That was his natural style both in and out of the courtroom. Which meant that he was not the best person to turn interesting facts into a compelling narrative. As Rose talked to him about ghosts, he imagined relaying the information to Olivia and hearing it sound about as captivating as a graduate-level lecture on cellular biology.

He did take notes, though. Lots of notes.

Gabriel had not yet told Rose the exact nature of the case. Even with a woman who made her living as a psychic, he feared he'd get as far as "hitchhiking ghost" and she'd burst out laughing.

In fact, her career made him even more wary. Rose wasn't some fortune-teller who honestly believed everything she told her clients. She might have the Sight, but she was also a Walsh, which meant she did some "filling in the holes" with her own carefully constructed fictions. Like Gabriel, she took the basic facts and massaged them into a pleasing narrative, one designed to make her point—whether it was that the client needed to give up smoking or kick out ungrateful offspring.

So he began by asking about vengeful ghosts in folklore.

Rose did not share his rhetorical style. Nor was she a psychic of the "wait, I see your future, slowly appearing, taking form before my eyes" variety. But the ability to tell a good story ran in the Walsh family, being one of the traits that had apparently bypassed him. So when he took notes, he made a concerted effort not to only record facts—as was his inclination—but to add the more colorful details for Olivia.

The vengeful ghost was a horror-genre staple, and for very good reason. If one was going to postulate the existence of spirits, it made sense that a reason they would return was to avenge a wrongful death. He'd had a case, years ago, involving a cat that did indeed seem to have nine lives, returning after each supposed death to stalk and torment his client—the cat's killer. Gabriel had even used that to convince his client to accept a plea bargain by giving him a choice: prison or the cat. He chose jail time. There are few things as pernicious as a cat that will not stay dead.

Vengeful ghosts, then, made logical sense. Cultures from around the world agreed, each having their own variation on the theme.

In ancient Rome, there were the *lemures,* angry because they'd been denied a proper burial, manifesting not in physical form but as a feeling of dread, of malignant darkness. China had a type of ghost that would make a defense attorney's job far more complicated: the *yuan gui*—ghosts with a grievance—wandering endlessly, looking for people with whom they could share evidence that would lead to their killers. China also had the *you hun ye gui,* seeking terrible vengeance on those who had wronged them. Japan had *onryō,* spirits returning for vengeance and not particularly concerned with whether they actually targeted the guilty, but acting in blind rage, causing natural disasters like earthquakes and drought.

Of particular interest for Gabriel's case were the stories of vengeful ghosts who returned to seduce men and lead them astray. He could see the sheer breadth of these stories as proof that such a very specific type of spirit must exist, but the truth was that one didn't need to dig far in folklore—as in life—to find examples of men making every excuse possible to explain an extramarital affair. If the folklore was to be believed, half the supernatural creatures in the universe existed solely for the purpose of tricking men into sex.

South Asia had an entire category of succubus ghosts: the *churel.* These were women who had been mistreated, often by their families, and wreaked vengeance by seducing and "draining" male family members, starting with the youngest. *Churels* could branch out, though, to find surrogate targets for their rage, and were known to wander lonely roads in search of men. And Venezuela had *La Sayona,* a beautiful young woman who was wronged by her family and exacted her revenge by seducing men and then either devoured them or "mangled" their genitals.

Female ghosts with long hair and white dresses also seemed a popular motif. China had the *nü gui,* wronged spirits with long hair and white dresses. Central America had the *Sihuanaba,* women with long hair and white dresses who would lure men away and turn around to reveal the face of a horse. Then there was the more generic "white lady" always with a tragic tale attached. She could be found around the world, and there were many regional instances where she would appear by a roadside, as the infamous ghostly hitchhiker.

"It would help if I knew what kind of ghost you were hunting," Rose said. "Apparently vengeful, but beyond that…?"

He told her the story. When she went still, precisely as he expected, he started to speak, but she beat him to it with, "I've heard this one."

"Yes, I am aware it is perhaps the most common of the modern ghost legends. I'm not concluding that is what we have, but the reports seem to make it clear we have something supernatural in nature."

"No, I meant that I'd heard this specific story. This legend. Twice, in fact. I had a client maybe ten years ago who claimed to have seen her. Then one in the past year. That's not unusual—I often see clients who believe they've had a supernatural encounter. Apparently, a psychic is the one person who might not laugh at you for that." She paused. "And I do try not to, though sometimes it is difficult. I had a woman last week who swore her new house was haunted…by ghosts running behind the walls, making chittering noises."

"Exterminator."

"Yes, and I'll work up to that suggestion after a few more sessions."

Rose reached for the last cookie. Then she stopped and motioned for Gabriel to take it. When he didn't, she moved the plate over in front of him and continued, "These two particular cases—of the hitchhiker in white—were among the more convincing. In the first

instance, the man was very distraught. He'd tried talking to his minister, who was very clearly out of his comfort zone, so someone suggested me."

"What was the nature of his encounter?"

Rose gave a story that matched many of the early reports—a young woman in white, a rainy summer night, an empty road. The man picked her up, but once she was in his car, she couldn't remember where she was going and began to panic and cry. He'd tried to calm her, promising to get help, but she'd disappeared.

"What upset him was, naturally, the encounter itself. He was the sort of man who, if he saw lights flicker, would contact an electrician, not an exorcist. But more than just being unsettled by the ghost itself, he couldn't shake the feeling that if she was a spirit, he'd failed to do whatever she needed to set her free. Over the course of a few sessions, I discovered he had a sister dealing with drug addiction, so we worked on addressing *that* issue, and he decided the ghost had been a manifestation of his feelings of powerlessness there."

"And it was?"

Rose refilled her tea. "One would think so, but I always got the sense there was more to it. That he had seen something, and it triggered guilt over his sister. His mind was looking for rational explanations. When I connected the dots, he could dismiss any foolishness about ghosts and focus on the real problem."

"Do you believe in ghosts?"

"I don't *dis*believe. I know Liv had what seemed to be an encounter, and I've met others who've experienced something similar."

"And you?"

She sipped her tea and said, "I've always thought that the greatest barrier to belief in ghosts is the fact we aren't overrun with them. If they exist, why don't we all see them?"

Which was not what he'd been asking, but he only said, "Presumably, it's the same as seeing the future or seeing omens. Some can; others cannot."

"So would a ghost like this stand on the roadside, hoping for someone who can see her?"

"I doubt she has more pressing engagements."

Rose gave a short laugh. "True. Which brings us to the second account. My second client. That one was…troubling. And quite different, despite the fact she described a very similar initial situation."

"Young blond woman in a sundress looking for a ride on a rainy night?"

"Exactly. The descriptions were eerily similar. Both of the young woman and her initial actions. But this one knew exactly where she wanted to go."

Rose related a story similar to Lambert's. Her client picked up a hitchhiker who said she was staying with a friend in the countryside, and it was perfectly fine for the woman to drop her off at the corner. Naturally, she didn't. And for her trouble, she ended up being led, like Lambert, down back road after back road, complete with a seeming loss of time, before ending up in the middle of an empty field. Whereupon the hitchhiker vanished.

"Did she say anything to your client?" Gabriel asked. "Before she disappeared?"

"No. But she was very agitated. The encounter had happened only a day before, and my client seemed to have come to me for reassurance that it wasn't real."

Gabriel's brows shot up.

"Yes," Rose said. "It might seem that a psychic is the last person you should ask that, but it's not that uncommon. When people have strange experiences, they either want me to validate or repudiate them."

"Because, as someone with a connection to the otherworldly, if you say ghosts *don't* exist, that's proof."

"Better than asking a priest or an academic. For those who want me to repudiate their experience—particularly with ghosts—it is often a matter of faith."

"They believe in a very different afterlife. Whatever their church promises."

"Yes, but in this case, she claimed not to be religious, not to have any reason for wanting me to confirm she hadn't seen a ghost."

"Yet she obviously had. As evidenced by her agitation."

"So I made a critical mistake, one that I seem destined to repeat, whether it's with a client or—" She glanced at Gabriel and then took a quick sip of her tea. "My mistake was in pushing. I could see she was distraught. I thought if I could get to the root of it…"

Rose shook her head and drank more tea before putting the cup down with a clack. "I couldn't, and in trying, I pushed her away. Which is really a lesson you'd think I—" She straightened. "She left. Then, I had a dream that suggested she was in danger. From herself."

"Suicide."

"Yes. I called the next morning, and when I couldn't get a response, I went into a bit of a panic. I was trying to find a home address when her mother phoned me back, having gotten my message. My client was fine, and I was not to contact her again."

"Which seems suspicious."

Rose chuckled. "Not at all. Imagine you had a witness who walked out on an interview, and her family told you to stay away. Would that be suspicious?"

"Not considering my occupation."

"Precisely. I've lost clients who *do* want to continue…and are convinced otherwise by family members. The same as I assume you have with witnesses. I did phone again, from another number, a week later, and got my client on the phone. I didn't try to talk to her—I just wanted to make sure she was okay. She was."

AS Gabriel was leaving, Rose handed him a box of cookies.

"For Liv," she said. "Take them across the road and tell her she forgot them."

Gabriel stared down at the box.

"It's an excellent excuse, Gabriel. Give her the cookies and clarify that her job is safe. Tell her that you're looking forward to seeing her at work tomorrow."

He tensed, his fingers tightening on the box.

"All right, then," Rose said. "Tell her you will see her tomorrow, and try to sound happy about it."

"I can say that I'm pleased she's back. Her workload has been accumulating and—"

"*No.* Please no. Just hand her the cookies and say you'll see her tomorrow. I bet she'll ask you in, and then you can tell her about the ghosts, letting her know you're still taking the case."

He checked his watch.

"Don't even pretend you need to get home. When is the last time you went to bed before midnight?"

"I meant that it might be too late to call on her."

"When's the last time *she* went to bed before midnight?"

He set the box on the hall table. "It would be inconsiderate, given her travels. I'll see her in the morning."

He let himself out, saying goodbye as her sigh trailed after him.

THIRTEEN

GABRIEL

GABRIEL ARRIVED at the office just before eight. Olivia was already there, at the filing cabinet, pulling out work. When he walked in, she fixed him with her brightest stranger-welcome smile and trilled a "Good morning" that sent his heart plunging.

She swung over Lydia's desk, perched on the edge of it and grabbed a box from the desktop. A very familiar box.

"I have brought cookies," she said. "Rose stopped by last night. She said you wanted to bring me some, but she forgot to make a box before you left. I've only eaten one. Possibly two."

She grinned, and Gabriel had to bolt his feet to the floor to keep from mumbling something, striding into his office and shutting the door. To keep from being inexcusably rude. To keep from making this worse.

Not that it could get much worse. She was acting...well, like herself. Classic Olivia. From the grin to the greeting to swinging over the desk, perching on the edge, joking about how many cookies she'd eaten. This was good-mood Olivia. Bouncy and playful. The side of her that he'd never quite learned how to coax out, like a sha-man trying to make the sun shine, realizing he could only wait, and it would come on its own.

This was one of his favorite sides of her, and so he should be happy. Olivia was back and acting like herself, and everything was fine. The sun shone again. Except it didn't. This was Olivia lighting a fire on the mountaintop and saying, "Look, sunshine!"

This was Olivia in fear for her job. Second-guessing herself, uncertain, uneasy. Very un-Olivia. And it was his fault.

When he'd offered her a position, he'd never stopped to consider the power dynamic it introduced into their relationship. His business had grown to the point where an investigator made good economic sense, and Olivia had the brains and the aptitude to learn the job. He also enjoyed working with her, which he'd always thought too much to expect of any employee.

Yet he was the one in charge. Assigning her tasks. Signing her paycheck. That still hadn't seemed a problem—it was a business arrangement that had no bearing on their personal equality. Or so it seemed until he'd gotten "pissy," as Ricky put it, over the Gwynn reveal. Gotten pissy and forgotten the imbalance of their work relationship.

Forgotten? No. A little honesty. Gabriel had known full well what he was doing when he told her not to come into work. Like a child who gets in a fight with a playmate and rescinds a sleepover invitation. *I don't want to see you. So there.*

Ricky had called him on it. He'd come to the office and spelled out exactly what Gabriel was doing. And Gabriel had ignored him.

I don't know what you're talking about.

You're misunderstanding the situation.

I'm very busy, and I have to leave now. Please let yourself out.

"Gabriel?" Olivia was still sitting on Lydia's desk. Still holding the box of cookies.

Your job is safe.

I'm sorry if I made you worry.

I would never terminate your employment.

She pulled the lid off the box and held them out. "Take one."

He did.

"I'll start coffee," she said as she swung off the desk.

Coffee.

Yes. He should ask her to join him for coffee. They'd walk to the shop down the road, and he'd buy her a mocha, and they'd talk about ghosts. He would tell her what Rose had said, and he would make it interesting.

He stood there, watching her brew coffee.

Too late now.

Really? It's coffee, not a four-course dinner. Just suggest getting her a mocha at the shop, and she'll gladly dump that.

"So what'll it be today?" she asked. "Black? Cream? Milk?"

"Black, please."

All right. Forget the coffee shop. Get her a mocha later. Just tell her about the ghosts. Sit down with your coffees and your cookies and talk.

He reached into his pocket and took out his notebook.

"I spoke to Rose about ghosts," he said.

"Oh?"

He thrust out the book. "It's in here. Read it, and then we can discuss. I have an appointment at eight-thirty, but I will be free after that."

He accepted his coffee with a murmured thank you and retreated to his office.

GABRIEL took his client in the meeting room, which meant Olivia had to clear out—that being the only other area to work in. When he emerged from his office, she was with Lydia, having already vacated the meeting room, as if to be sure she didn't delay his appointment even a nanosecond. He motioned for her to work in his office, and she zipped past without a word.

Once his meeting ended, he opened his door and set her scrambling to gather her papers and laptop, even though she'd been working at the side desk—the spot where she used to sit, sharing the space with him.

"Leave it," he said, gesturing at her things. He pointed at his notebook, now on his desk. "Are you done with that?"

"I…I wasn't sure what you wanted me to do with it," she said.

He frowned. "Read it. Transcribe, if required. I said we were going to discuss it."

"Yeah…" She settled back into her seat. "Last time we spoke, you told me to drop it."

"No."

"You were clear on that, Gabriel. But okay, so you've changed your mind?"

"No."

"If you're giving me those notes so I can moonlight as Patrick's research assistant, I hope that doesn't imply a reduction in my hours." A bit of the old Olivia seeped into her voice. A note of steel that warned it had better *not* mean that. "You've been telling me how busy you are, so it's not as if you don't need the investigative work."

"I do. And I am not implying that you should moonlight for Patrick. What I meant is that I did not intend to suggest I was dropping the contract."

"*Suggest* isn't really the word you want there, Gabriel. You said—"

"I was tired. Irritable. Anything I say under those conditions should not be taken at face value."

Her lips twitched. "Can I get that in writing?"

He lowered himself into his chair. "I will admit that I'm torn by this case. I don't need the money. Nor will it bolster the professional reputation of my firm. It is, in short, a zero-sum proposition."

"But it intrigues you."

He made a face. "That's hardly a good reason—"

"It's the best reason. If you've earned the money and the rep, then this is your reward: the chance to solve a puzzle for pure interest's sake."

"One always needs more money and a better professional reputation—"

"Want. Not need. Two different things. And you'd like to solve this, right? It interests you."

"If it interests *you*…"

She sighed. Deeply. But she also relaxed in her chair, the conversation having slid back toward the realm of normal for them. "Fine, fine. Yes, you know I find it interesting. But don't use that to pull your bullshit."

"My bullshit?"

"Where you pretend you're indulging my whim so you can whine about it later."

"Whine?"

"Grumble. If you want us to pursue this, then we pursue it. If you can't be bothered, then say, *I can't be bothered.*"

She watched him and waited.

After a minute, he said, "My current schedule does allow the addition of this contract, and I believe that the historical aspect may prove useful for both of us, as a research angle we don't often encounter in our cases. It would not be a complete waste of my time."

"Close enough." She reached for his notebook. "So let's talk about ghosts."

FOURTEEN

PATRICK

PATRICK SAW Gabriel's Jag backing from the alley beside his building, and he broke into a jog, pulling up beside the car and rapping on the driver's window. It rolled down with a "Yes?"

The voice did not sound at all like his son's, and it took another moment to actually look and see a young woman in the driver's seat, one with ash-blond hair and green eyes, her lips pursed, as if she'd bitten into something and found it not to her taste.

"Liv?" He paused. "Why are you driving Gabriel's car?"

"Shhh. I'm stealing it. Now, if you'll excuse me…"

He jogged around the back of the vehicle, which may not have been the wisest choice, as he could swear he heard her playing with the accelerator. She kept her foot on the brake, though, at least until he'd cleared the bumper, and then she let the car roll back. He grabbed the passenger door and managed to get it open and slide in.

"What are you doing?" she asked.

"Adding kidnapping to the charges."

"Excellent. Now I just need to commit murder, and I'll have a full crime-spree hat trick."

"Still angry with me, I see."

"Not angry. Annoyed."

"You threaten to murder people who annoy you?"

"I'm part fae. I can't help myself. What do you want, Patrick?"

He looked out the side window. "Where are we going?"

She turned onto the next street. "If this is about that ridiculous project you set Gabriel on—"

"You don't like it?"

"Oh, I like it just fine. What I don't like is you sniffing around, trying to ingratiate yourself with him."

"Sniffing around? That sounds vulgar."

"No, just desperate." She took another corner, a little too sharp, smacking him against the door.

He fastened his seat belt as he said, "Are you forgetting that I saved you from Tristan?"

"No, you only 'saved' us from the inconvenience of figuring out what to do with him, and you only did that for this very same reason: to ingratiate yourself with Gabriel. Possibly me, too, as Matilda, but it's mostly about Gabriel. Which is why you started coming around while I was out of the country. Doing an end run around me."

"That is...unfair."

"Can barely get the word out, huh?"

Patrick settled back in his seat. "You're the one who is so upset about me failing to play a role in my son's life. Now that I am, you're angry with me. You need to make up your mind, Liv."

She hit the brake so hard he was grateful for the seat belt, though he still might have bruises later.

"Out," she said.

"It's not your car."

She steered to the curb, yanked the gearshift into park and got out. The door slammed. The trunk opened. A clatter as she took something out. Patrick envisioned Liv marching around to the passenger door with a shotgun. Instead she marched past with a parcel under her arm.

He took off after her. As soon as his door shut, she lifted the key fob and hit the lock mechanism without turning around. He jogged to catch up.

"You do remember that I carry a gun, I hope," she said, and he had to smile. It wasn't as dramatic as pulling a shotgun on him, but still...

"About the case," Patrick said. "I have reason to believe it's actually a ghost."

"Well, duh."

"I'm quite serious, Liv."

"So am I. Sure, there's a possibility it's not, but all signs point in that direction."

"No, I mean it really is a ghost."

She glanced over her shoulder at him, brows knitting. "Did I miss something? Because from what Gabriel said, you've been arguing that all along. He thought it was a fae, posing as a ghost, and you're the one who claimed it was an actual ghost."

"Yes, but..." He looked up and down the quiet street. "Where are we going?"

She lifted the parcel.

"I don't see a post office," he said.

"It's another block. I was getting fresh air. The kind that doesn't reek of hobgoblin."

"You should be glad I appreciate your humor, Olivia. I wouldn't put up with that from anyone else."

"It has nothing to do with my sense of humor and everything to do with the fact that I am Matilda. I'm useful to you, and you're useful to me. But I think the balance weighs in my favor, and right now, yes, I'm pissy about you doing an end run around me to pester Gabriel with a pointless case."

They turned the corner. And there was the post office. Patrick waited on the sidewalk until she returned and then fell in step beside her. They walked in silence for a while, then he said, "I need you to do me a favor."

She laughed. He waited until she'd finished. It took a while.

"I would consider it a large favor, Liv," he said. "Which means a large favor owed in return. And I'm counting my help with Tristan as a freebie."

"No one asked you to help with Tristan."

"Gabriel came to me for advice on dealing with a spriggan."

"Okay, great. I'll let him know that you consider *that* a favor owed, which means he will never bother you for advice again."

"My reference help—for either of you—is freely given."

Another laugh. Almost as long. Then she said, "It's not freely given when you keep reminding us of that. And it's not freely given when it helps position you as an ally to both Matilda and Gwynn."

"I want you to tell Gabriel that you're no longer interested in this case."

She looked over. "The case you *gave* him?"

"Just tell him that you hit a dead end. You found a snag in the theory. You uncovered evidence to suggest it's all a scam. I'll make up the story. You only need to convey it."

"So…lie to him. Awesome. Because he deals so well with me *withholding* information that he's bound to be even happier if I outright lie. Should I tell him you *aren't* his father, too? That if he hears anything to the contrary, just ignore it?"

"You're free to tell Gabriel that I'm his father, Liv. I'm happy to give you that."

Her glare sent a chill through him. "You mean you're happy to lay that responsibility on me."

They reached the car. She strode to the driver's side. He waited for the click of the door lock and jumped in before she could stop him.

"I don't want you pursuing this case," he said. "I'm worried about both of you."

She pulled the car from the curb. "Do I dare ask why?"

"Because it's a ghost."

She growled under her breath.

"It's a real ghost," he said. "Yes, I know I told Gabriel it was. But I was... Well, I lied. I'm a bòcan. We do that."

"You lied about—?"

"You were right. I wanted an excuse to get to know him better. I brought him this case because I knew it would interest him, and I thought we could work together on it."

"Didn't quite turn out that way, did it?"

Patrick sighed. "No."

"Because Gabriel doesn't work with anybody. Which you'd realize if you knew him."

"He works with you. He trusts you, and you have his best interests at heart, which is why I'm opening up here and confessing that, yes, I tried to get to know my son better, and if that's a crime—"

"It should be."

He gave her a look, but she said, "I'm serious. I think there should be a statute of limitations for absentee parents. Once the kid hits eighteen and no longer needs you, you are forbidden from making contact and fucking up his life."

"*Fucking up?* I know you're angry, Liv, but I have done nothing of the sort."

"No? Bringing him a fake story just to get his attention? Leading him on a wild goose chase with it? And then, once he's intrigued, telling *me* to stop him. Because Gabriel and I are on *such* good terms right now. There's no way that could *possibly* blow up in my face."

"I'm just worried—"

"About this ghost. Why? What's dangerous about ghosts?"

"I don't know. Which is why they're dangerous."

She made that noise again, the one that warned this conversation better improve or he'd find himself flying out of a moving vehicle.

"I don't know anything about ghosts, Olivia," he said. "That is troubling enough. And this one gives me a bad feeling. A very bad feeling."

"Then tell him that."

"He'll think I have an ulterior motive."

"Wow. Really. I don't know why." She pulled up in front of Gabriel's office greystone and tapped the horn. "I'm not quitting this case, Patrick. I can't—not without Gabriel thinking I'm being petty and bratty, still upset over what he did."

"You *are* still upset over what he did."

"No, I'm resigned. This is what I get with Gabriel. This is what I will always get. I'm the idiot who keeps doing the same thing over and over and expecting a different result. I've finally learned my lesson. That doesn't mean I'm abandoning him. I'm just easing away."

"He doesn't want you to ease away, Liv."

"Don't."

"I just—"

"You do have an ulterior motive here. Gwynn is the Tylwyth Teg champion. You're Tylwyth Teg. So don't even go there. My point is only that I don't want to make things worse between Gabriel and me, which I will if I drop this case. If you want it dropped"—she put down the window—"tell Gabriel yourself."

A shadow stretched through the driver's window. "Tell me what?"

Liv got out of the car, and Gabriel said, "You can drive."

"No, she's yours."

"You're welcome to—" Gabriel turned as if watching her walk away. "You are coming, aren't you?"

"Of course. I set up the interview. You aren't stealing my witness. I believe there was also the promise of a mocha."

Patrick winced. Listening to Olivia was like hearing the understudy in the lead actor's role, trying to emulate the original but falling short. It sounded like Liv; it was not Liv. And as Patrick climbed out, he could tell Gabriel knew it.

"You wished to speak to me?" Gabriel said to him.

"I was…I, uh, was telling Liv that you guys need to be careful. With the ghost."

"All right…"

"I don't know much about them, and maybe this research isn't all that important for my book. In fact, I'm thinking of going in an entirely new direction."

"If that is an attempt to avoid paying your bill—"

"I'll pay. I'll write you a check right now. And then you're done. You can get back to your regular work."

Sunglasses covered Gabriel's eyes, but Patrick could still feel them fixed on him. Looking for Patrick's angle, certain he had one. Then Gabriel glanced toward Liv, getting into the passenger seat, and with that Patrick knew he'd lost. Gwynn's Matilda had come home to him, and she wanted this. She wanted the case, and she wanted to work with him. That was enough.

Gabriel opened the driver's door. "Lydia will send your bill along with a report of our findings to date. If you wish to know any further details on our investigation, you will have to ask her to reopen your file, at the agreed-upon rate."

FIFTEEN

GABRIEL

GABRIEL AND Olivia had arrived at the apartment of one Angela Vogler. Twenty-six years old. Elementary school teacher. Currently home for the summer.

Fourteen months ago, Ms. Vogler had been driving along a rural highway outside of Chicago. She'd been returning to the city after breaking it off with her fiancé. Despite her emotional turmoil, she'd stopped upon seeing a young woman at the side of the road. A blonde in a white sundress.

Ms. Vogler was Rose's former client. The one who'd fled after a second session. The one Rose had a prophetic dream about, suggesting Ms. Vogler might be a suicide risk. Yet she was, fourteen months later, still alive and, moreover, had agreed to see them.

As Olivia made the introductions, Ms. Vogler turned to Gabriel and said, "You look like your aunt," with a small smile that suggested this was not cause for alarm. Had it been, Olivia would hardly have linked their story to Rose.

"As I explained on the phone," Olivia said, "Gabriel's aunt, whom you know by her professional name of Rosalyn, has been threatened with legal action. We're hoping to compile enough contrary evidence to convince the plaintiff not to file suit. The best way to do that isn't to gather statements from satisfied customers, but from those who expressed dissatisfaction."

"Like I said on the phone, I wasn't dissatisfied. I just...I decided a psychic wasn't right for me." Her cheeks reddened. "I shouldn't have gone to one in the first place. It's not really my thing." She glanced at Gabriel. "No offense to your aunt. She was super nice. It just wasn't for me."

"I know that Rosalyn contacted you after you left," Olivia said. "Your mother wasn't pleased by that, and we're concerned it could be misinterpreted as a predatory practice. Calling to lure you back."

"No, no. It was clear she was just checking up. My mom can be a bit protective. And psychics really aren't her thing either. But Rosalyn only asked how I was doing, and she never called again. She didn't even bill me for the session I walked out on. I was ready to pay. I can still do that."

"No need," Olivia said. "But we would like to ask a few questions about the nature of your visit. Anything you tell us is in complete confidence. Once we hear your story, we can determine whether the complainant's lawyer might try to call on you as a witness."

Ms. Vogler's eyes rounded. "A witness? In a lawsuit?"

"We're trying to make sure it doesn't go that far," Olivia said. "And if it does, then the more you can tell us, the less likely it'll be that you'll be summoned. Now, we have some idea what you spoke to Rosalyn about, but she wanted to protect your privacy, so we'll need to ask for the full story from you."

Ms. Vogler's version matched what Rose had told Gabriel. She'd come to Rose for reassurance that what she'd seen on the road that rainy night had not been a ghost.

"Which is obvious, right?" Ms. Vogler gave an embarrassed laugh, her hands fluttering. "It just—it seemed so real, and I had to know. I was just..."

"Compelled?" Olivia said.

Ms. Vogler nodded. "Exactly. This overwhelming compulsion to get an answer. To have someone tell me I didn't see a ghost. I know it sounds silly..."

"Unnerving is what I'd call it," Olivia said. "You try to help someone, and she not only took off but tricked you into thinking you saw a ghost. I'd want answers, too. Preferably the kind that said I didn't see a ghost."

Ms. Vogler smiled. "That's it. Except in my case, it wasn't a prank, either. It was a manifestation of my anxieties. That's what my fiancé says. He's getting his doctorate in psychology."

"Fiancé. Congrats. Rosalyn mentioned you'd had a breakup that night. Is this...?"

"Same guy." Ms. Vogler flushed. "We worked things out."

"Ah, so *that* was the anxiety being manifested. About the breakup."

"Not...exactly." Ms. Vogler picked at a thread on her skirt. "The breakup was...fallout from other...issues." She turned to Gabriel. "Your aunt helped me see that. Please thank her for it. I was in a predicament. One I wasn't even acknowledging to myself. Let's just say something happened to me, and I hadn't acknowledged it, and I needed to. She helped me do that."

"I'm glad to hear it," Olivia said. "So when you say that the supposed ghost was actually a manifestation of your anxiety, I'm guessing you mean it was your subconscious prodding you to make a decision."

"Yes."

"And prodding you in what way? Did the hitchhiker refer to the incident in question?" Olivia paused, and Gabriel could see her struggling to find a way to tie this to their cover story. "Did you share something with Rosalyn that she failed to pick up on?"

"No, the message wasn't that obvious, which is why I didn't understand it myself. The ghost—or whatever I thought I saw—said I was lost."

That old chill slid down Gabriel's neck, and he heard himself repeating, "Lost?"

Ms. Vogler glanced over. "Yes. She said I was lost, and I had to find my way back on track, and if I didn't…"

The schoolteacher trailed off and swallowed.

"If you didn't?" Gabriel prodded.

"Then I should end it. I should just end it."

SIXTEEN

GABRIEL

"IS THIS case making any sense to you?" Olivia asked.

They were in a coffee shop. It wasn't one they'd visited before, but Olivia had a sixth sense for them, particularly the trendy sort with comfortable seats, empty at this time of day, as people headed home, having imbibed sufficient caffeine.

Olivia had apparently not imbibed sufficient caffeine—or sugar, having added a brownie to her mocha. Now she alternated between solid and liquid chocolate as she tapped her pen against her notepad.

She had asked a question, but he knew he wasn't supposed to answer. Not yet. She was still working it out herself.

"We have forty years of one very specific type of ghost. Sad Christina who can't find her way home. And then, *boom,* vengeful-demon Christie." She looked up at him. "This better not be a demon."

"I have no evidence that such a thing exists."

"Excellent. I'll seize on that as proof and totally ignore the fact that, until a few weeks ago, you didn't know ghosts or fae existed either." She wrote "Not a Demon" on her pad and double-underscored it. Then she skimmed her notes. "I'm missing something."

"We both are, because I fully agree that our ghost story has continuity issues."

"So something happens two years ago that sets her on the path to vengeance. Maybe people stopped picking her up? Or someone mocked her and sent her over the edge?" Olivia sighed. "I'm really grasping at straws."

"Then let's focus on the current iteration of Christina Moore. We have two confirmed suicides, both occurring forty-eight hours after their ghostly encounters. Lambert kept telling me he had forty-eight hours to find his way. But he didn't know what that meant."

"Nor did Angela Vogler at first. She only knew that she felt a sense of urgency to resolve her issue. An urgency so strong that she responded by instead trying to prove she hadn't seen a ghost—in other words, no ghost meant no timeline meant no penalty. It seems to only have been after she fixed her problem that she gradually remembered what the ghost had said."

"Yes."

"So Ghost Christina doesn't care about getting home anymore. She's turned her afterlife attention to playing therapist-from-hell. The ultimate motivational speaker. You have forty-eight hours to fix your life, or you have to *take* your life. That's some seriously tough love."

"Vengeance is a theme with some of the ghosts on Rose's list. Particularly the sort of vengeance we saw with Lambert. They target men who are unfaithful to their wives, luring them away and then killing them."

"Forever wreaking blind vengeance on the men who betrayed them." Olivia wrinkled her nose. "Male ghosts seek vengeance on whoever wronged them, whether in business, in battle, or in their personal lives. With the women, though? It's all country song, he-done-me-wrong."

"Not in Ms. Vogler's case. I'm presuming that the breakup was precipitated by infidelity on her part. She was either unfaithful or considering it."

Olivia shook her head. "Sorry, counselor. That would be an incorrect interpretation of the facts. She said something happened to her, and refusing to acknowledge it was sending her life into a tailspin. That's not her doing something—it's something being done *to* her. Physical abuse. Sexual harassment. Assault. Either happening at the time or something she'd recently remembered."

"Like an incident of childhood sexual abuse."

"Right. The memory returns. She tries to deny it. Life goes haywire, culminating in Angela breaking up with her boyfriend for some unrelated reason— fallout from the stress. That would make Angela a victim, not a perpetrator. So Christina is not a vengeance demon."

Gabriel tapped the "Not a Demon" in her notebook. That made her laugh.

"Yep, that covers it. Doesn't explain what we have, though. Why would a ghost target people who need to fix their lives, even if it's not their fault? In the case of Lambert, I'm not even sure there *was* something wrong in his life. He just wasn't appreciating what he had."

"True."

"But that could apply to people in so many areas of their lives. Maybe the ghost doesn't *know* what's wrong with these people. Maybe she doesn't even sense that there is something wrong. It's like omens and superstitions. Walk under a ladder, and later that day, stub your toe and, hey, it must have been the ladder."

"In other words, the ghost plants a thought, and her victims determine what it means."

"That's what they are, isn't it? Victims." She tapped her pen against the notebook. "Christina has become a predator. And the best way to catch a predator? Set a trap."

Two minutes of silence passed.

"That doesn't help, does it?" she said. "Not unless our 'trap' is waiting for a rainy night and driving every back road outside of Chicago in hopes she'll appear."

"Hmm."

"Which means you don't have any more plausible ideas."

"It means that I admire your resolve and your determination, but yes, trapping the ghost isn't feasible."

"So we've hit a dead end?"

"Possibly."

"Damn."

OLIVIA had dropped the case. There was no disagreement precipitating that decision. Gabriel wished there had been. He could fight that, leveraging her obvious interest to lure her back in. But no, the case had simply fizzled out.

There was no place left to go, and normally, she would never let that stop her. Quitting was surrender. But this case was different. The trail had grown cold, and there was no reason to push on. The client had withdrawn his support. There wasn't even a victim to save. Future victims, possibly, but as Olivia said, "We aren't ghostbusters." Which meant partly that they had no skills for stopping a ghost and partly too that they were not movie heroes, fighting injustice simply because it was the right thing to do.

Olivia needed actual motivation. At the very least, she needed a mystery. Yet they'd solved that. Christina Moore had died and, as Olivia put it, she'd rechanneled her phantom energies into a new career in extreme life coaching. Mystery solved. Mostly. The question of *why* remained, but Gabriel would be the first to argue that motivation rarely mattered in a criminal case. In this instance, they knew she was guilty...and could do nothing to stop her.

Which made for a very unsatisfying conclusion.

The next day being Saturday, Gabriel was free to try to reopen this particular investigation. Search for the tidbit that would pique Olivia's interest again.

He was not, of course, completely free. He didn't base his schedule on a five-day forty-hour workweek. To him, evenings and weekends simply meant that his time was his own, untethered to meetings and interviews and appointments. He spent the morning working on legal cases, and in the afternoon dove back into their ghostly one.

Olivia had uncovered a possible third suicide, the connection to the ghost more deeply buried than the others. Gabriel dug deeper into all three cases. It was dull work, as such research often was. Rather like having pieces of a jigsaw dumped onto your desk and being told to make something of it, without even being certain all the pieces comprised a coherent whole.

He spent hours moving the pieces of data around, trying to find where they might connect. And by the time he found something, there was no thrill of victory, but rather the gut-level awareness that he really was, as Olivia put it, grasping at straws.

All three obituaries of the deceased victims listed "Greater Chicago Suicide Prevention" as one charity to which mourners could make donations in the name of the deceased. The fact that all three used the same foundation wasn't outwardly odd—no more than three cancer victims using the American Cancer Society. But if one is going to grasp at straws, one ought not to do so halfheartedly. So Gabriel researched the charity. What came back was the American Foundation for Suicide Prevention: Greater Chicago/ Illinois Chapter. Quite a lengthy name when one might be restricted by an obituary word count. "Greater Chicago Suicide Prevention" must be the accepted short form. Except it wasn't—he found only two other obituaries using it...and both in the last two years.

He made a note of the names. Then he searched specifically on "Greater Chicago Suicide Prevention" and found only the website linked to it in the online obituaries. It was a very professional design, but only a single page, with a commitment statement and a donation form. The commitment statement was what you might expect. Suicide was terrible. Losing someone to suicide was terrible, too. Let's all work together to help suicidal people find better solutions. Nothing connected that website to the American Foundation for Suicide Prevention.

A records search followed. It took some digging, but he finally found an address for the charity. What he did not find was anything suggesting it *was* a registered charity.

And what did that mean? He had no idea, but he did have an address.

SEVENTEEN

PATRICK

PATRICK CLIMBED the steps of the three-story walkup, the only multiresidence building in Cainsville. On the stoop, he found the usual suspects: a cat and a boggart, actively ignoring one another. The boggart was Grace, the building owner, wearing her cranky old lady glamour. Well, the "old lady" part was a glamour. The "cranky" part was just Grace.

"Is the lady at home today?" Patrick asked as he crested the steps.

"You'll have to be more specific, bòcan. Which lady?"

"The only one who counts."

Grace sniffed and grumbled under her breath. Whether that grumble was directed at Liv or him, Patrick couldn't tell. Both probably.

He turned to the cat. "Hello, TC. Would you tell your master I've come to call?"

TC fixed him with a stare only slightly less baleful than Grace's.

"You expect that'll work?" Grace said.

"He's a *matagot*. Which means he understands me just fine."

"He's also a cat. Which means he doesn't care."

"I just want to talk to Liv. May I cross your threshold and call on her? Or would you like to fetch her for me?"

"I'd like you to leave her alone. She doesn't have time for your game."

"What game?"

"Whichever one you're playing. Now go, bòcan, before I—"

The front door opened. Liv walked out. "Hey, TC. You keeping Grace company? That's so sweet." She turned to Grace. "Don't worry—I'll bring him in when I get back. I'm grabbing coffee at the diner. And a scone for you, naturally."

"Tea, too."

"Yes, ma'am."

Liv walked right past Patrick and headed for the walkway between the buildings.

"Take a hint, bòcan," Grace said.

"Never," he said and hurried off.

When he caught up to Liv, he said, "That's terribly rude, you know. Ignoring me when I came to talk to you."

"I thought you came to talk to Grace. I didn't want to interrupt."

"No one comes to talk to Grace." He matched Liv's strides. "I know you and Gabriel aren't taking my advice about dropping this case. So I'm offering my help."

She said nothing. Just kept walking.

"Free help," he said. "Whatever you need. No strings attached."

"There are always strings attached."

"All right then. I do have a motivation. I'm concerned about this ghost business, and I want to protect you and Gabriel."

"Matilda and Gwynn, you mean."

He said nothing for a few steps, as he fought the urge to defend himself. To get annoyed, even. To tell her not to trivialize his concern or deny him the right to be concerned.

Except she was correct in her way. She might not know the full history behind the situation, but he could not deny that he'd made mistakes. Endlessly compounded mistakes, culminating in her very understandable mistrust.

He had to remind himself that her anger wasn't *at* him. It was *for* Gabriel.

"I'm worried," he said finally. "Whatever the reason. If you insist on pursuing this, I want to help."

They reached the end of the walkway and veered toward the path leading to the diner. Liv had stayed silent as they passed the playground.

"Have you found anything new?" Patrick asked.

She said nothing.

"Are you investigating today? I didn't see Gabriel's car."

"He's working at home."

Patrick felt a frisson of alarm. "Alone? On the case?"

"On other cases. Legal work."

"So you're investigating the ghost on your own? That's not good, either."

It wasn't as bad as Gabriel investigating alone. The unease he felt about the ghost situation centered on Gabriel.

"I'll be fine," Liv said. "Gabriel's busy, and I want to make progress on this. Surprise him." She shrugged and said, "Impress him," and there was this note in her voice that made him look over, but she was looking straight ahead, no hint of anything untoward.

"I was thinking of going to the cemetery tonight," she said, in that same casual tone.

"Cemetery?"

"Hey, how often do I get the excuse to poke around a graveyard at night? Gotta let me have my fun."

"Is Gabriel joining this excursion?"

"That would spoil the surprise. It could also be really embarrassing, pulling him away from his work to pursue a whim. I'm going to try to contact the ghost. With James…" She cleared her throat. "Suffice to say, I think I've seen ghosts before. It may be an extra on my Matilda-vision package. I'm going at night because it'll be quiet, which might help with the ghostbusting."

"Gabriel panics over you having visions at any time. What is he going to say about you going to a cemetery—alone—for that express purpose?"

"Awesome initiative?"

Patrick glared at her. "No, he will not. And you're not. I'm going with you."

They headed into the passage beside the diner.

"Olivia…?"

"I don't need the backup."

"I can help. Backup plus research. I might not have much on ghosts, but I'll find what I can. I have resources."

She pursed her lips, and with that gesture, a little too dramatically thoughtful, Patrick realized he'd walked into a trap.

Liv hadn't been going to the diner for a coffee. She must have a perfectly good coffeemaker at home. She'd been going because it was the most likely place to bump into him.

She wanted his help with this. Not that she'd have said so. Oh, no, she'd have given the same performance at the diner. Ignore him, knowing he'd want an update on the ghost case. Play him a little, making him work for details. And then oh-so-casually mention that she planned to try contacting the ghost…to impress Gabriel.

Impress Gabriel? No. This was about going behind Gabriel's back to do something he would forbid. Yes, she *would* impress him if she made progress in the case, and that was always a factor in the careful dance between them. Partly about impressing the other, but more about proving themselves equal partners, worthy of each other's attention. Not unlike the mating displays of many species, though Patrick doubted they'd appreciate the comparison.

They'd hit a dead end with the case, and Liv wanted to break through it, but her only idea was one that Gabriel would hate. She knew better than to do it alone, and while Ricky might seem the obvious partner, that made him equally culpable. Liv didn't particularly care if Gabriel got angry with Patrick. And Patrick's research skills and fae abilities would be an added bonus.

"All right," she said finally. "You can help. If you insist."

"I do."

EIGHTEEN

GABRIEL

IT WAS past six, afternoon stretching into evening. Gabriel had not heard from Olivia. He hadn't expected to. But hoped? Yes. He'd hoped that she would wake up this morning and seize on some new avenue to pursue in the case, perhaps even one as far-fetched as his, proving he wasn't the only one desperate to mend this rift. But he knew better. She'd given him chances. One after the other. He'd used them up and not only continued making mistakes but—never one to rest on past successes—he'd made each worse than the last.

He would fix this, though. He would. Starting with this case. He just needed a valid lead to lure her back.

He looked up at the building before him.

This was not a valid lead.

It was an office building, of exactly the sort one might expect to house a small charity foundation. Not suspiciously downtrodden or suspiciously ostentatious. An older building, in much worse shape than his own. While his greystone might not be in the most prestigious neighborhood, it had dignity and history, perfect for a successful independent lawyer. He'd chosen it for that very reason... and the fact that he'd gotten a significant discount by offering a lifetime of legal advice to the former owner, who'd run a meth lab out of the basement.

There were no meth labs in this building. There were lawyers, though. He noticed several plates as he walked down the hall. No names he recognized. It was not that sort of building. Rather, it was exactly the sort he'd been determined to avoid—the sort that said you'd only opened your own firm because you weren't good enough to join a large one.

It was a three-story walkup, like Olivia's. No elevator. Which gave him the excuse for wandering, noting the types of occupants. Three lawyers. Two accountants. A graphic designer. A "lifestyle coach"—which gave him pause, thinking of Olivia's joke about the ghost, but a box of pamphlets attached to the door suggested it was actually what it advertised. Still, in Gabriel's opinion, that was one business where one clearly should have a more prestigious address. Same went for the person down the hall advertising his services as a stock analyst. It was hardly good advertising for such businesses to be in a building like this.

The office he wanted was on the third floor. Up there, he found fewer professionals and more offices not intended to receive visitors, discreet signs noting the business name only for deliveries.

At the end of the hall, he found the number he wanted, on a door marked "Pigsie Industries." He double-checked the address. It was definitely the one attached to the suicide prevention charity.

An Internet search on Pigsie Industries brought back no hits in the Chicago area. It was an odd word, childlike. He searched on that alone. Google suggested he meant "Pigsy," and he informed it that he did not. But what returned for Pigsie *or* Pigsy was nonsense. Fictional characters and online names and such.

And there were no hits for Pigsie Industries at all.

When he examined the door more closely, he noticed the camera and cursed himself for missing it. From this side, it looked as if the door had a peephole, like the others, yet this one was slightly different. That prompted a closer inspection, upon which he determined that it was actually an eyehole camera.

Gabriel was retreating when he heard a click from inside the office. He put his ear to the door. Another click. The camera? Or was someone inside?

He knocked. He'd already been seen by the camera, so he might as well rap and hope someone opened the door and gave him a glance inside as he made a "wrong address" excuse.

No one answered his knock.

Another click sounded. A mechanical one. Then silence. He strained to hear.

Nothing.

One last look around, and then he left.

GABRIEL was eating dinner in the kind of place he did not eat dinner. Or any other meal. Apparently, it was vegetarian. He'd missed that detail, noting only that it looked like a healthier choice than the surrounding fast food shops.

He was not particularly fond of fast food, but it was—as advertised—quick. Which meant that he ate it more often than he should as a cheap and efficient way to refuel. He could blame habit from his years on the street, but even before Seanna left, Gabriel had had to buy his own food, and he'd learned to make healthy choices. A banana and milk would get his body farther than fries and a Coke. His recent fast food habit was pure laziness...and a major factor contributing to that soft middle he was trying to fix in the gym.

So while vegetarian would not be his first choice, he stuck with the restaurant, if only because finding another would be inefficient.

As he ate, he considered what he'd discovered. Was the records address for the charity incorrect? That wasn't impossible, but Gabriel suspected otherwise. He was a Walsh; he'd smelled a con from the moment he'd clicked on the website for Greater Chicago Suicide Prevention. Both professional and bland, it looked like exactly what a con artist would post to seem like a real business while not giving away anything that could be traced.

So a false charity had preyed on all three suicides, along with two others. Olivia had already raised the near-certainty that there were other victims. People like Angela Vogler, who hadn't reported their "phantom hitchhiker" encounters. He suspected, then, that the two other obituaries listing Greater Chicago Suicide Prevention as their charity marked two more of Christina Moore's victims.

But what did that mean? A con suggested a human con artist. There was no doubt that the victims had encountered a supernatural being. People didn't disappear in the blink of an eye, and if they seemed to, then you were sitting in the audience of an illusionist, watching a well-rehearsed stunt on a well-designed stage.

Could it instead be hypnosis? Or some other form of mind control? They had experienced that already, but it had used a sprinkling of "fairy dust."

And where would that conclusion lead? Why would someone be randomly targeting people and trying to induce them to kill themselves, only to achieve a success rate of approximately twenty percent? To win a few thousand dollars in donations?

There were easier ways to make money. Far easier and far more profitable for a con artist of this caliber.

So what *was* the answer?

Gabriel had no idea, but he knew where to start looking.

NINETEEN

PATRICK

"ALL RIGHT," Liv said as Patrick climbed into her car. "I have everything you told me to bring. We are ready for a séance."

"A séance in style, I see," he said. "I've heard rumor of the Maserati, but I haven't seen it. Spyder?"

"1961."

He whistled. "Yet you insist on driving that old Jetta? I'm disappointed."

"This is my dad's." She paused. "*Was* my dad's." Another pause. "My adoptive father."

"And I'm guessing he didn't leave it to you?"

"No, he did. A garage full of classic sports cars bequeathed to his speed-demon daughter."

"So the reason you drive the Jetta?"

Her hands tightened on the wheel. "Ready to go ghostbusting?"

"You need to segue topics more smoothly, Liv."

"No, that was just a polite way of saying it's none of your business. There's a list of the séance ingredients right there. Can you check and make sure I brought everything?"

He scanned the list. "You forgot the proton packs."

"The *what?*"

"You're the one who made a *Ghostbusters* joke. Please tell me you've seen the movie."

"When I was, like, five. I remember a giant Marshmallow Man. I wasn't supposed to bring marshmallows, right?"

He sighed.

"Well, they'd probably be as useful as the rest of this stuff," Liv said, "considering you couldn't get any actual information on actual ghosts from your supposedly actual contacts. We're relying on folklore here. Which is like solving a mystery using techniques from a detective novel written by a twelve-year-old."

"Maybe, but the twelve-year-old has to have gotten those techniques from somewhere."

Liv turned the corner. "We call it 'imagination.'"

"Not entirely. Even a child cannot create literature in a vacuum. It's influenced by her experience of the world. Her detective story would include nuggets of true detective work, from shows she'd seen, books she'd read…"

"Because law and order in real life is *just* like on the TV show."

"It's a fictional version based on reality. Which still means you can dig and strike truth." He waved the list of supplies. "That's why this is so long. I'm not saying it'll *all* work. But something in here will help. It must. And if all else fails? We have Matilda."

TWENTY

GABRIEL

GHOSTS.

That was what Gabriel had found. He stood in the corner, his heart slamming against his ribs, the way it hadn't since he was a boy, in genuine terror for his life, fleeing one of Seanna's boyfriends after she blamed her son for money she'd stolen.

True fear. Visceral and real and almost enough to send him flying from the room. Shame, too, because these ghosts here weren't the sort who could whisper compulsions in his ear and make him kill himself. No, these ones whispered to his psyche and made him doubt himself, made him feel as if everything he'd accomplished was no more substantial than the dust in this room. Blown away with a breath, all his old fears exposed.

Where will I sleep?

What will I eat?

How will I live?

Will I live?

He was back in that room where he'd met the woman fifteen years ago. It was dark outside—it'd taken time to find the building, wandering through what he knew had to be the right neighborhood. Finally, he'd stopped trying to remember where it'd been and let his feet lead, and he'd wound up here.

The building was no longer abandoned but seemed under reconstruction, another desperate effort to revive it. Yet what Gabriel saw was the original, half-ruined room, and a boy with a backpack, the memory as sharp as one of Olivia's visions.

He watched the boy poking around. Calm. Determined. Resolute. *Seanna has left. Ah, well. It was bound to happen sooner or later. No time to feel sorry for myself. Push on. Make the best of it.*

That's what he saw. Calm and fearless resolve. A child who had never been a child. Propelled into adulthood too fast and now pushed off the edge, sink or swim, and the look in his eyes said sinking was not an option.

That's what he remembered. It was not, however, how he felt, and being here, all the rest came rushing back. The fear. The terror. The panic that he could not do this, that however tough and self-reliant he thought he was, this went too far. Seanna may have been the worst possible mother, but she'd provided stability. A source of shelter and normalcy, allowing him to attend school and pretend he was just a regular kid with a mother who put dinner on the table every night.

Now she was gone, and he honestly thought he could carry on as he had? Go to school? Graduate? Get into college? Get into *law* school?

Gabriel watched himself poking around the room, trying to decide if it was a suitable shelter for the night, acting calm and steady while feeling utterly lost.

You will get there. You will.

The boy turned and looked at him. *And then what?*

The question startled Gabriel, and he pulled back.

No, really. And then what? I get the degree and the career. I get the fancy condo and the fancy car and the stocks and bonds and investments. And then what?

Security. That's what he would win. That's what Gabriel had always wanted. And he had it.

Great. Makes us happy, I see.

It made him secure. Comfortable. Comforted.

Eating fast food dinners by yourself. Awesome.

Was he implying Gabriel needed a lover? Gabriel snorted at the thought.

Never said a lover. Just someone to eat that dinner with. Those things we call friends. You had that with Olivia. Liked it. Fucked it up. Keep fucking it up. Can't help fucking it up because Seanna didn't let us have friends growing up. So we never learned how.

That was an excuse. Gabriel did not make excuses.

Right. But it's not an excuse. It's fact. Accept it. Work past it. Like we did out here. Seanna left. We worked past it. Another obstacle to overcome. Not an excuse. Don't let it be an excuse. Remember what you said to that lady in here? You weren't lost. Don't get lost now.

The boy faded, and Gabriel stood there, thinking of what he'd said. Not the part about friendship. He knew that—the boy was a projection of his own mind and hardly going to tell Gabriel anything he didn't already know.

What caught his attention was the mention of the lady. The reminder of why he was here—for the same reason he might return a client to the scene of the alleged crime. A trick for sparking across the severed wire of a mental connection. In Gabriel's gut, he knew there was a connection between Christina Moore's ghost and the woman he'd seen that night. He'd known that before and failed to pursue it. But now with the added wrinkle of the fake charity, his subconscious nudged him back to that connection.

His subconscious?

Or Gwynn?

Gabriel twitched. It didn't matter. Wherever the nudge came from, it brought him here. Back to this place, and if he reached into his memories again, he could conjure up the woman, aided by the sight and smell of this room.

He closed his eyes, and when he opened them, she stood there, a mental reconstruction, ready for examination. Peasant blouse and long skirt, rather than a sundress. White, though, if he wanted to make that link. White with pale blue flowers, if he wanted to make that *distinction*. Hair light brown, not blond. Long and flowing, though, like Christina Moore's. Also like another image he'd seen.

His aunt had brought out her books for him to let Gabriel skim the entries on ghosts. He remembered making a note for Olivia about the preponderance of female ghosts described as "dressed in white with flowing hair." Those ghosts that had led men—and sometimes women—astray, quite literally, posing as lost women and luring unwary travelers deep into the wilderness. Sometimes seducing them. Sometimes killing them. Sometimes just leaving them to find their own way home.

For what purpose?

Therein lay the problem. In the cases of vengeance, one presumed the ghosts were driven by that insatiable need. In the cases of sex, perhaps that need was insatiable, too. But in the others, did the ghosts simply lead people astray for fun? Gabriel might say motivation didn't matter, but it did help. He seemed to have found it in that fake charity, but no ghost could set that up, and both Lambert and Angela Vogler picked Christina Moore out of a photo lineup, and there was no way the answer was "Christina Moore is alive and conning people" when she'd be in her seventies now.

He examined again the woman he'd encountered here, all those years ago. She was clearly not Christina Moore. Yet her talk of being lost and getting back on track echoed what Christina had apparently told her victims, and it felt like more than randomly homogenous platitudes.

He saw the woman, and he heard her words again, trying to lure him away. A similar woman trying to achieve a similar purpose.

Find the connection.

His phone vibrated, and he snatched it out, as he'd been doing all day, hoping to see Olivia's text. It was just another client seeking an update. He felt the urge to reply that it was ten p.m. on a Saturday night, but that never went over well. Best to just pretend he didn't get the text until Monday morning.

As he closed his messages, his browser screen reappeared with its search on Pigsie.

There's more here. Something you missed. You know there is.

No, he did not know that. But something deep in his brain did, and he'd pretend it was his subconscious and not Gwynn.

Yet thinking of Gwynn—however much he'd rather not—did accomplish one thing: it sparked another connection. Another possibility. One that worked far better than the square pegs Gabriel had been jamming into this round hole.

Gwynn. Legendary king of the Tylwyth Teg. King of the fae.

Fae.

When Patrick first brought him this case, Gabriel had proceeded with the presumption the culprit was fae, no matter how much Patrick swore otherwise. Then along came Christina Moore, seeming to shout that Patrick had been right all along.

Not fae. Ghost.

Or was she?

Gabriel typed pigsie and fairy into his browser. This time, Google gently suggested he really meant pigsy, but it did not attempt to force his hand. His browser screen filled with those results, starting with a dictionary definition.

Pixie. Otherwise known as pixy, pisky and, in some areas, pigsie.

He continued typing in search terms until he found exactly what he was looking for. Again in the dictionary, no less.

Pixie path: A route which bewilders and leads astray anyone who follows it.

The term dated back to folklore. Fae lore. The idea that pixies would find travelers and get them lost. There was even a term for it. Pixie-led. To be confused. Bewildered. Literally, to be led astray by pixies.

Gabriel tapped Olivia's number.

I have the answer. Well, no, not exactly—there are still missing pieces—but I have an answer. One that you'll like. One you'll want to pursue.

We are officially back on the case.

It took four rings. Gabriel was ready to hang up and call back, in case she was temporarily delayed from answering. Then the click that signaled the line had connected, but it took another three long seconds for her to answer, and even then, it was a tentative, "Hello?"

"It's me. Where are you?"

Another pause. "Am I supposed to be somewhere?"

"No, no. I have something to discuss, and I was wondering if you were in town."

"I'm…" Pause. "At home."

"All right. I'll come there."

"No," she said quickly. Then, "It's late."

"It's ten o'clock."

"Here it is. But it's midnight Atlantic time, and I'm still adjusting."

No, she was making excuses. Why...? Yes. There was one scenario where Olivia would be reluctant to have him visit late in the evening.

"Ricky's there," he said. *And presumably spending the night.*

"Uh...ye—"

"No, wait, I saw him earlier, and he said he was working for Don tonight. Did that change?"

Pause. Pause. Pause.

"He had Saint's business," she said. "I'm just really tired. Is it something we can discuss on the phone? Or tomorrow?"

"No, it's fine."

His words came out clipped, and she said, "I'm not trying to blow you off, Gabriel. It's just—"

"You're tired. We can discuss it another time."

"Tomorrow?"

"Monday will be sufficient. I'll see you then."

"Gabriel, wait. We can—"

"It's nothing. I'll see you Monday."

He disconnected before she could protest. Then he closed his eyes. When he opened them, the boy stood there, backpack on his shoulder as he shook his head.

Well, that went well.

Gabriel turned his phone off.

You feel rejected. Even the tiniest thing like that, and you take offense and reject her before she can hurt you. Call her back. Text her. Say tomorrow will be fine. Invite her to breakfast.

Gabriel pocketed his phone. He would see Olivia on Monday. He could tell her about the pixies then. He wouldn't interrupt her weekend any further.

The boy sighed. Gabriel dismissed him and strode to the door.

TWENTY-ONE

PATRICK

PATRICK WATCHED Liv exhale as she hung up the phone.

"Well, that went well," he said, backing up to perch on a headstone.

She glared at him.

"Could you have made it less obvious that you were blowing him off?" he said.

"I couldn't concentrate with you flailing over there."

"Flailing? I was trying to signal directions."

"Directions for an incoming plane, it looked like."

She walked to the headstone and knelt in front of it. "I should call him back, shouldn't I? Tell him the truth. Maybe he'd like to come out. Join this fiasco of a séance. Couldn't hurt."

"Oh, yes it could. Imagine how that call goes. *Hey, Gabriel, I'm in the cemetery, trying to summon a ghost. Wanna play?* No, Gabriel does not want to play ghostbuster. Nor will he want you playing ghostbuster. Did you tell Ricky what you're doing?"

She shook her head.

"Rule of thumb?" Patrick continued. "If you think it's too dangerous to tell Ricky, don't even *think* of telling Gabriel. I'll handle any fallout from this. I'll tell him I offered to help only if you let him enjoy his Saturday night in peace."

She straightened. "This isn't working anyway. I should call Gabriel back and ask if he wants to meet up. See what he had to say."

"No and no. We've been at it barely an hour. And it's ten o'clock. Hardly the witching hour."

Her finger brushed the phone in her pocket.

"No," he said. "Now come over here and—"

A pale figure slipped between two tall monuments.

"Did you see that?" he said.

Liv sighed and slumped to the ground, leaning against Christina Moore's gravestone.

"I'm serious." Patrick pointed. "Didn't you see her?"

"Nope. Not this time. Not the last two either."

"I saw *something* before, not a figure." Okay, *lied* about seeing something might be more accurate. He had to keep her attention somehow, not unlike a small child who wanders off after five minutes of playing catch. The problem was that Liv wasn't a small child, meaning by the third time, she'd caught on. Just when he'd actually spotted something.

Patrick headed that way. "It was a pale figure. A woman, I think."

"Wait…"

He stopped and smiled. See, that wasn't so difficult.

"Wait," she said again. "I see her, too. A pale figure in the darkness, walking 'in beauty, like the night / Of cloudless climes and starry skies; / And all that's best of dark and bright—'"

"You know Byron. Wonderful. But you know what? I actually knew him. Partied with him a few times."

"Why am I not surprised?"

"Oh, but I bet I know things about him that *would* surprise you."

"Not unless they prove Byron wasn't a total dick."

Patrick thought. Thought some more.

"Yeah," Liv said. "Figured as much. If you want to impress me, tell me you knew Mary Shelley."

"Yes! I did know Mary. In fact, I was there on that fateful night when Byron proposed they all write ghost stories, and the monster of Frankenstein was born, an entire genre of fiction arising from the pen of a young woman— "

"Wait, did you see that?"

He gave her a hard look. "If you aren't interested, just say so."

"I am interested—if it's true, which I doubt." She got to her feet. "But I saw a figure over there. Among the taller statues."

"Pale figure of a woman? Like the one I *told* you— Where are you going?"

She waved him to silence and took off at a slow lope toward the larger monuments. He hurried to follow. If he'd told her not to bring Gabriel into this, he was responsible for keeping her safe.

Patrick remembered the last time Liv fell into a vision trance at his instigation. He'd been a little less concerned than Gabriel liked, perhaps made a comment that had been...unwise given his son's agitated state.

Gabriel had hit him. Not a shove or a smack, but a fist out of nowhere, knocking him to the floor. And Patrick had been impressed, both by the skill of the strike and the sheer balls of it, no trepidation in hitting a fae, no fear of repercussions.

Fae preyed on trepidation and fear, and once they scented it, they lost all respect. So Patrick had been pleased. Not that he could admit that. He'd warned Gabriel against ever doing it again, and fully expected—and hoped—his son would ignore that with other fae.

Right now, though, Patrick remembered that blow and hurried to catch up with Liv. She was pulling away fast as she slipped between headstones. Once she reached the large ones, he lost sight of her for a second and broke into a run, whispering, "Liv!"

She reappeared on the other side of an angel and motioned for him to be quiet. She gestured emphatically at a spot out of his sight. Then she hunkered down and began creeping forward.

A figure passed between headstones. A young woman with long blond hair, wearing a pale dress. Liv crouched behind a large family monument, watching the figure as it slipped through a stand of trees, moving into an older section, more park-like, with towering trees.

Patrick snuck up beside Liv.

"You saw her, right?" Liv whispered.

He nodded. Liv started out. He tried to grab her back, but she was already on the move, sneaking between the large family markers, headed for that wooded area. She got a few steps and then paused, her head tilting, as if listening to something.

As Patrick drew up beside her, he frowned, gesturing to ask what she heard. She pointed to her feet and made a stomping motion. He arched his brows.

"Footsteps," she mouthed.

When he listened, he heard the patter of footsteps coming from the direction the young woman had gone. Liv seemed to be waiting for him to make some connection, but he only shrugged. She mouthed, "Ghost?" He still didn't get it. She threw up her hands and started forward again. He stayed right behind her now, moving from one hiding place to another and—

"Woooo," a girl's voice said.

Patrick may have jumped. Liv did not. Her eyes narrowed, and she looked in the direction of the voice.

"Woooo." The spine-tingling sound floated over on the night breeze. Or it was spine-tingling to him. If Liv's eyes narrowed any more, she'd be walking blind.

"Woooo—"

"Gotcha!" a guy said.

A girl shrieked, and someone else said, "That was the lamest ghost noise ever, Em. Seriously. *Woooo?* Please tell me you're already loaded."

"Not yet," the girl said. "Someone pass the bottle, and I'll get started."

"Shhh," another girl said. "I heard someone out here earlier. We need to keep it down."

"Beth's right. Wouldn't want to spook the spooks."

Liv kept creeping until they were close enough to see the speakers. Four kids, maybe college age, sitting on a blanket, enjoying a cemetery picnic. One of the girls had long blond hair and wore a pale blue sundress.

"There's our ghost," Liv muttered and then began to retreat, grumbling under her breath.

Patrick fell in at her side and whispered, "It might not have been her the first time."

"It was."

"Then we need to keep trying. We know Christina Moore's ghost has been wandering about, and all the folklore for ghosts is very clear that if you summon them at their graveside—"

"The folklore is also clear that to stop a ghost, you have to dig it up and burn the bones."

"Uh, no." He paused. "You've been watching *Supernatural,* haven't you?"

She kept walking, pulling away now. "My point is that the lore is full of crap."

"We'll keep trying," Patrick said. "The night is young. Those kids aren't the only ones with a bottle. I brought wine. *Fae* wine."

That made her slow. He smiled behind her back and said, "Never had fae wine, have you? It might help with your visions."

She turned to face him. "You mean wine that fae use to induce permanent hallucinations in humans?"

"I wouldn't say *permanent.*"

She spun on her heel and stalked off. He jogged after her. When his foot hit an embedded gravestone, he stumbled. As he righted himself, he heard Liv say, "What's—?" Then the pound of her footsteps as she broke into a run. He looked up sharply and saw a figure, just a few feet away. The figure of a young woman in a white sundress running for a mausoleum, with Liv in pursuit.

Patrick ran, whispering, "Wait! Don't—"

And they both disappeared.

TWENTY-TWO

GABRIEL

GABRIEL STRODE down the empty street. When he saw a shadow recede into an alley, he ignored it. This was that sort of neighborhood. While they might take a look at the cut of his suit and declare him a worthy target, he knew how to deal with this sort of predator. He'd had more knives pulled on him than he cared to recollect. A few guns, too. Little ever came of it. He hadn't been mugged since he was a boy.

But when he ignored the shadow, the boy in his head whispered, *Stop*. Gabriel ignored that, too. He was done here. There were no real ghosts. Not Christina Moore and not the irksome ones from his past.

Irksome?

He glanced down the alley. No one was there. The shadow had been a trick of his imagination.

You have no imagination.

He snorted at that and carried on. When he reached the next alley, he turned to walk down it. He'd parked nearly two miles away, and while he might feel safe, that confidence did not extend to the safety of his vehicle.

As Gabriel turned into the alley, he saw a man standing about ten feet away, blocking his path. He slowed but didn't stop. Stopping suggested fear.

He couldn't see the man well, any light from the street swallowed by the tall buildings. The man seemed average in size. Blond hair. Bearded. Nothing menacing in his stance. He simply stood in Gabriel's path.

"I told you to stop," the man said. "When that didn't work, I thought this might."

Gabriel pulled up short. His gut clenched, as if reflexively, and he peered at the man, but more than just darkness hid him. The figure seemed half-shadow himself, seen through a veil of swirling fog.

Gabriel squeezed his eyes shut, forcing this particular phantom away. The man sighed, and when Gabriel opened his eyes, the figure had become the boy from earlier—the reflection of himself, backpack and all.

"Is this better?" the boy said. "It's all the same, you know. Him, me, you. All memory. All you."

Gabriel opened his mouth to respond and then realized the preposterousness of speaking to an external representation of his subconscious.

"Oh, go ahead," the boy said. "In this neighborhood, people talk to themselves all the time."

Gabriel took out his phone.

"Checking messages?" the boy said. "How about accepting the one we're trying to transmit. You're being followed."

Gabriel flipped through screens.

"Not even going to look around, are you? You already know you're being followed."

Obviously, he did, at some level, or this externalized manifestation wouldn't be telling him that. But that's what he would expect around here. A scavenger prowling until he decided Gabriel didn't look like easy prey.

"Are you sure that's it?"

Gabriel kept flipping through screens on his cell phone.

"Oh, I get it," the boy said. "You aren't ignoring me. You're giving yourself an excuse for stopping and listening. All right. I'll shut up."

Thank you.

The boy vanished, and Gabriel was left in that alley, pretending to search for something on his phone while calling on his powers of deep perception, the ones that had nothing to do with any preternatural ability and everything to do with years spent in neighborhoods just like this, his senses attuned to every sound that could signal trouble.

He half-turned, as if questioning his route. As soon as he did, he sensed someone stepping into the alley. He lifted his phone and switched to the camera. It took him a moment to find the button to reverse the direction of the lens. He remembered Olivia teasing him about that, saying, *"What? You don't take selfies and post them to Instagram?"*

"I only know what Instagram is because it was pertinent to a weapons offense I defended. The victim made the mistake of posting photos of my client's parrot to his account, which led—It's a long story. Quite dull, actually."

"Oh no, don't pull that crap, Gabriel. Tell me the story. Now."

Gabriel shook off the memory. It took effort. He kept seeing her expression, green eyes glittering, eager to hear whatever madness he was about to impart. There was nothing momentous in the story or the memory, just one of dozens, those easy moments of conversation, relaxed and content and, yes, happy. Pleased with himself and happy. Such a small thing, and yet not small at all.

Focus.

He shook it off harder and lifted the camera. And there, behind him, was a woman, one who looked exactly like Christina Moore.

Exactly? No, he misspoke. The alley had not suddenly grown brighter. Yet he could see her better than he'd seen the figure of the man, and there was little doubt that she appeared to be the woman from the photo, right down to her white sundress. As for whether it *was* Christina, that was another matter entirely .

When he took a step her way, she fled down the alley. Gabriel broke into a jog. He reached the alley end and looked around to see an empty street. No sign of—

A flash of white between two buildings. He jogged over to see a narrow road. A homeless man sat on the curb. Gabriel strode over and wordlessly held out a twenty. The man pointed down the road and gestured left.

Gabriel set out and made a left just in time to see Christina dart down yet another alley.

She's leading you.

Yes, he realized that.

She's trying to get you lost.

Yes, he realized that, too.

You should call Olivia. For backup.

He didn't need backup.

It makes a good excuse.

He ignored the voice and continued until he reached the alley. A door stood half open partway down, and he shook his head. She might as well have posted a Welcome sign.

He moved carefully, loafers rolling with each step. When he reached the door, he considered. Then he stepped through.

The door led into a hallway of closed and numbered doors. Offices? Apartments? He couldn't tell. He took a few steps, listening for sounds of life from behind those doors. Silence.

When his phone buzzed, he quickly took it out and saw Patrick's name. Gabriel hit Ignore and stepped to one door. No peephole. A keyed lock. No deadbolt. He slipped a thin glove from his pocket and tried the knob. It turned.

His phone vibrated again. A text from Patrick.

Urgent. About Liv.

Gabriel released the doorknob and retreated. He closed the door, making sure it would still open. Then he called Patrick.

"*What* about Olivia?" he said when the bòcan answered.

"Hello to you, too, Gabriel."

"*What* about Olivia?"

"I need you to calm down."

"And I need you to tell me what this is about, or I will grow steadily less calm, culminating in angry."

"Mmm, I think you're already there."

"Culminating in vengefully angry. What is—?"

"I've misplaced her."

"Mis—?"

"We came to the cemetery to summon the ghost of Christina Moore."

"*What?*"

"Everything was going fine, until Liv, well, vanished."

"Are you still at the cemetery?"

Patrick exhaled, as if relieved that Gabriel hadn't started ranting. He felt like ranting—at Patrick, at Olivia, at himself even for jumping to the conclusion she was blowing him off earlier. Yes, she had been, but it'd been trickery rather than rejection, and he'd been having far too much fun sulking to realize that. But shouting and snarling wouldn't get Olivia back. Directions would.

Patrick confirmed that yes, he was still there, and Gabriel strode from the building, wondering what his chances were of summoning a taxi faster than he could get to his car. In this neighborhood, not good.

"It's a vision trance, isn't it?" Gabriel said as he walked. "She brought you for backup, meaning she wouldn't wander off. Not far, anyway."

"Yes, it seems to be a vision. She was following the ghost of Christina Moore, and then, gone. Both of them."

"It's not Ms. Moore."

"Maybe, but it definitely looked like her, and it was a ghost, so I'm going with the most obvious solution. Considering we were trying to summon Christina—"

"Ms. Moore is not a ghost."

A pause. "She's alive?"

"No, I'm saying that this hasn't been her ghost. It's a pixie."

"Pixie? No, Gabriel. We're dealing with a ghost. All the evidence—"

"—has been misconstrued. It's a pixie. And I believe she's here, attempting to lure me somewhere."

"Wha—? *No.* I have no idea *what* this is, but if you think you're being pixie-led, get out of there. Do not pursue."

"I'm not. I'm coming to you. I'll call when I'm close."

Gabriel hung up. He shoved the phone into his pocket and turned the corner, onto the street and—

And he was not on the street. He was in another alley.

He looked behind him to see an alley. He'd stepped from one into another, which made no sense at all. He could not be at the juncture of two—

But he was. He must not have been paying enough attention as he initially followed the pixie, and he'd walked from one alley to another without realizing it.

No matter. He'd continue down this one and—

He turned the next end to see yet another alley. And the homeless man on the curb. As Gabriel walked by, the man lifted a grimy ball-cap and peered at Gabriel with impossibly bright green eyes.

"You lost, sir?"

Gabriel looked up and down the alley.

"No, I don't believe I am."

"Then you're wrong, Gabriel Walsh." The man smiled up at him. "You're very, very wrong."

TWENTY-THREE

PATRICK

PIXIES? REALLY? Well, no, not really. Patrick remembered when Freud came out with his theories, and suddenly everything from bedwetting to homicidal rage could be explained by an unhealthy love for one's parent. That's what Gabriel was doing. He'd discovered the existence of fae, and so everything inexplicable could be explained by that.

Patrick shook his head as he continued walking through the cemetery, searching for Olivia.

Gabriel must have done an Internet search on "fairy" and "lost" and gotten "pixies." You would really think a lawyer would know to be more critical with his online research. Yes, if this were fae, a pixie would fit, but if Patrick honestly believed it could be one, he'd be a lot more worried.

Pixies were one of the most malicious subspecies. Oh, sure, they got great press—probably the result of some forward thinking when humans first came into contact with fae. *Let's make ourselves look as cute and innocuous as possible!* Fae overall had done that well—with the exception of subspecies like his own—but none had managed it better than the pixies.

Pixie dust. Pixie sticks. Pixie haircuts. Magical. Sweet. Childlike. The terms associated all that with the creatures themselves, as tiny and innocent fae. Which could not be further from the truth.

Most fae subspecies enjoyed a good prank. Those ranged from harmless to annoying, rather like human ones. For a prank to turn cruel, a person had to deserve it. Pixies, though? They started with cruel and worked up.

But this wasn't a pixie. It was Christina Moore, who could not *be* a pixie. Patrick had investigated that possibility when he first learned they actually seemed to be dealing with a ghost. Could Christina have been a fae, who appeared to die and came back? No, she had a human family and a birth record. She had been human. And she had died. And now she'd come back—as a ghost, not a pixie, which would be all kinds of impossible.

Speaking of impossible...

Patrick peered around the darkness.

No Liv here. No Liv there. No Olivia anywhere.

He wasn't too concerned. He'd called Gabriel mostly to cover his ass. Liv's vision states were just one of her Matilda powers. They pulled back the veil for her, not unlike his live-action reference books. She stepped in and saw something—past or present—that helped her understand her situation. Sometimes she lost consciousness. Sometimes she wandered beyond the veil. Gabriel might panic over the fevers, but it made no sense if visions meant to help her could also prove lethal. Nature didn't work that way.

Patrick would, however, like to find Liv before Gabriel arrived. Present her to him, safe and sound.

If I were a ghost, where would I go?

That was hardly helpful. If Patrick were a ghost, he'd go every place he couldn't otherwise. He'd peer into lives he could never inhabit, see people in their realities rather than the projected images they showed for others. As a ghost, he imagined he could spend centuries just listening and observing. That was the writer in him.

Christina Moore was not a writer. For a musician, she didn't even seem terribly imaginative, given that she was a ghost lurking in a cemetery.

Patrick checked his phone. Nothing. As he glanced up, he caught movement over by the mausoleum. A flash of white, like the flip of a dress as someone fled.

He jogged over to the mausoleum.

"Woooo," a voice whispered from the other side. "Woooo." Then there was a giggle. A drunken giggle.

Patrick grumbled under his breath and turned to stalk off.

"Woooo!" More giggling, followed by a snicker.

All right, if these kids wanted to play ghost, he'd show them how it was done. Give them a fright to send them fleeing so he could concentrate on finding Olivia.

"Woooo!"

Yeah, yeah. He walked to the mausoleum. Reached up. Sighed when his fingertips fell a few inches short of the edge. A quick look around before he shed his glamour. An easy scramble up the wall. Then he kept his true form as he crept to the other side, where he could hear the girl snickering. He glanced over the side and—

A girl leaped at him, her face a mask of blood, cheek torn and flapping.

Patrick let out a yelp. More like a squeal, but he was sticking with the less humiliating "yelp."

As he fell back on the roof, another figure swung up onto the roof. A familiar figure, grinning a familiar grin…until she saw him and let out a yelp of her own.

"Holy shit," Liv said, scrambling back. "Patrick?"

He glowered at her. "Who else?"

That's when he remembered he wasn't wearing a glamour. He cast his as fast as he could.

"Thank you," Liv said. "That is one creepy glamour."

"It's not—" He bit off the protest and settled for a deeper scowl.

"Wait? Is that your real look? Freaky green spider monkey?"

"Monkey? Did you see fur? No. It's not—"

"Olivia?" a girl's voice called.

"Hold on. Just helping my friend here recover from his heart attack." Liv crawled over and looked down. "Your death mask is awesome, by the way."

Patrick moved to the edge as Liv lowered herself beside… Christina Moore. Wearing a sunny dress and a sunny smile and no trace of blood or gore.

"Sorry if we spooked you," Christina said as Patrick climbed down.

"Totally my idea," Liv said. "That's Chrissy's death mask—her face at the moment of her death."

Patrick glared at Liv. "So while I've been searching in an absolute panic, you've been making friends with a murderous spirit."

"Panic?" Liv snorted. "You were enjoying a leisurely stroll among the tombstones. And none of the dead are Chrissy's fault. Seems she's been the victim of afterlife identity theft. Someone—*something*—stole her likeness and her backstory and trapped her here while the imposter goes all deadly phantom hitchhiker."

"Imposter?"

"Fae, I'm guessing. I hate to jump to that conclusion, but if it's a nasty-ass prank, it's gotta be fae. Do you know of any—?"

"We need to get to Gabriel. *Now.*"

TWENTY-FOUR

GABRIEL

THE HOMELESS man's face changed, reverse aging until he looked about Gabriel's age.

"Aren't you going to ask how we know who you are, Gabriel Walsh?"

"There are too many possibilities, and it hardly matters how. You do. As for how you found me, it would be the camera at your office. When it detected a figure, it sent an alert and, presumably, an image, which you recognized. Then you were able to track me here. Being pixies, with the power to make people lost, I would assume you can also find them."

"Oh, but you are clever," said a voice behind Gabriel. "Just not clever enough to avoid that camera."

Gabriel turned. Behind him stood a young woman who was undeniably Christina Moore. She smiled, and her form seemed to ooze, features reconstituting into a dark-haired young woman. Another glamour. Which ought to be impossible. Most fae possessed a single one, which they could age up or down as they desired. None could impersonate another person. Yet clearly she had.

Gabriel said, "If I avoided the camera, you wouldn't be here, and I would have to hunt you down. This is easier."

The pixies laughed. There was, however, a thread of uncertainty woven through it. Not that Gabriel had any clue how to turn this situation to his favor. He just couldn't let them know that.

He took out his phone and checked it.

"Waiting for something?" the male pixie said.

"Nothing of import," he said, in a tone that suggested otherwise. "Now, I would like to discuss the matter of Christina Moore."

The female pixie feigned a yawn. "Dull. Let's talk about someone else. His name starts with a *G*. Not Gabriel, though. What was your mother even thinking, naming you after the opposing team?"

When he didn't reply, she prodded, "Gabriel's Hounds? It's another term for the Cŵn Annwn."

"I prefer to think she named me after the archangel, as befits my saintly disposition."

When they hesitated, Gabriel discreetly texted Patrick: *Tips for dealing with pixies?*

"What are you doing?" the male asked.

"Checking my stocks. I'm thinking I might want to drop any interests in Pigsie Industries. I hear they are about to suffer a setback."

Silence. Then the male snorted, "Oh, that's good. Clever Gwynn."

If Gabriel tensed at the name, the pixies failed to notice, and the female said, "One of our kind met you years ago. Or so she said. Gwynn ap Nudd, the greatest king the Tylwyth Teg have ever seen, reborn as a street boy seeking shelter in abandoned buildings. Others thought she was telling stories. I knew it was true—proof of how far the Tylwyth Teg had fallen. Their king, a dirty-faced boy rooting around in trash cans."

Gabriel could say he never ate from the garbage, but the truth was that he'd come closer than he cared to admit. Instead, he only shrugged. "Isn't that one of Gwynn's titles? The warrior with the blackened face? I was simply fulfilling my destiny. Now, about Christina—"

"Let's talk about Gwynn. Do you know who he is to the pixies?"

"Nothing, I presume, as you are not Tylwyth Teg."

The pixie blinked, as if he'd stolen her punch line.

"No," Gabriel said, "That's not entirely correct. I am something. I am useful. That's why you've waylaid me."

"We waylaid you to tell you to get out of our business, which is not Tylwyth Teg business. We want you to remember that."

"That's what you seek, then. A pardon from the king, for this and all future transgressions committed on his lands."

"This is not your land," the female spat.

"Of course it is. In asking me for diplomatic immunity, you acknowledge the territorial rights of the Tylwyth Teg as extending beyond Cainsville—"

"We didn't ask for diplomatic immunity."

"You've asked me to allow you to conduct your business on what is presumably Tylwyth Teg territory or you would not ask —"

The female pixie flew at him. The male lunged to hold her back.

"No," Gabriel said. "Let her do as she wishes. At worst, she might kill me, but it's not as if I won't return, in another time, in another form. Which is more than I can say for either of you when the Tylwyth Teg avenge my death."

"You think you're protected, boy?" the female said. "It's true we don't dare harm you. But we haven't harmed anyone. You humans do that all by yourselves, and if you decide to put a gun to your head two days from now, do you think anyone will question it? Do you think anyone will care?"

His shoulders tightened before he could hide the reaction, and her lips curved in a smile.

"They'll care about Gwynn," she said. "But you, Gabriel Walsh? No. There's nobody to care, is there? Nobody to mourn."

He told himself it didn't matter, but that was a lie. A lie for the man he'd been. A lie for the man he'd tried to be.

But he would not go unmourned. Rose would care. And Olivia, as unsteady as their relationship might be right now. Perhaps others, but those two were enough for him to know the pixie's words should be easily sloughed off. One moment of self-doubt and then a sneer for her poor effort.

But as he told himself it wasn't true, his breathing quickened, doubt seeping in. Was he certain about Rose? Perhaps she'd mourn at first but then be relieved, no longer tied to him, no longer forced to pick her way carefully through the minefield of their relationship. Olivia, too. She would miss him at first, but then perhaps feel relief, Matilda finally freed of Gwynn and his endless betrayals. Freed to live her own life.

Gabriel gritted his teeth. It was as if the pixie had reached inside him and found the tender spots beneath his armor, as if she knew exactly where to poke and prod and release the fears of a child. He looked into her eyes and saw them glitter, working whatever magic she possessed.

"I'm fine," he said through those gritted teeth.

"Oh, no, Gwynn, you are not. You've lost your Matilda. Again. Rather tiresome, isn't it? To keep *needing* her. To keep losing her. To feel lost without her."

"I'm fine."

The female smiled. "You keep telling yourself that, Gwynn."

"I don't need to. I know it. I am fine. Yes, I lost my way, but I'll find it again. I always do. I don't need Olivia. I *want* her in my life, but that's an entirely different thing."

The pixie's eyes narrowed, and her mate made a noise, like a growl.

"I cannot offer that boon you requested," Gabriel said. "I'm in no position to do so. But I am willing to negotiate. If you leave Illinois, I won't pursue you for the crimes you've committed here."

"Crimes?" the male sneered. "We've toyed with humans. That's what we do. It's what all fae do. If you plan to stop that, Gwynn, then you have a lifetime of disappointment ahead because it's like vowing to clean up the ocean, one grain of sand at a time."

"I'm not concerned with the ocean. I'm concerned with you. Here. Now. Stop killing humans."

"One more," the female said.

"No more."

"Oh, I'm afraid you don't have a say in the matter, Gwynn. One more. And then we will stop. You have our word."

The male reached up and grabbed him by the hair, wrenching so fast that Gabriel didn't have time to react. His head snapped to the side, and the female put her lips to his ear and whispered, "You're lost, Gabriel Walsh. So terribly lost. But you can fix it. You know how to get back on track. How to end this. End it for good." Her voice lowered. "You have one hour."

Gabriel blinked. Then he rubbed his neck and looked about.

"What am I doing here?" he said.

The female smiled. "You know, Gabriel. Tell me what you have to do."

"Fix things. End it."

"Exactly."

He frowned at her. "Exactly what?"

The pixies chortled.

"One hour," the male said. "Best get moving."

Gabriel texted Olivia, asking her to meet him…

He looked around. "Where are we?"

The male fae leaned over and typed an address into the text message. "That will get her close enough."

"That's very helpful," Gabriel said. "Considering she's coming to help me stop you."

The female smiled. "No, she's coming to help you, Gabriel. Help you get back on track. And we can't wait to see it."

TWENTY-FIVE

PATRICK

PATRICK GRUMBLED as he stalked down the alley. He'd been left out. Again.

Oh, yes, Patrick, please help me contact this ghost. Please watch my back. Now, when the fun starts, run along and play.

Okay, that wasn't exactly how it happened. But that's how it felt.

Gabriel had texted him—*him*—to ask how to deal with pixies. Not Liv. Patrick. Had he gotten a thank you for his response? For his reassurance that darling Olivia was fine? Not a word. Instead, Gabriel switched to texting Liv. Plotting with Liv. Telling her that he had the pixie and needed her help capturing it.

How was Liv supposed to help? Patrick was the expert.

To be fair, Liv had noted the oversight and realized Gabriel presumably meant for Patrick to sneak up another way and do the actual capturing while she and Gabriel distracted the pixie.

It was the "sneak up another way" part he was grumbling about. They'd split up, and Patrick had followed Gabriel's directions—to the letter—and wound up at a dead end. Worse, he had no idea where Liv had gone. He'd texted Gabriel twice without a response.

He'd finally broken down and texted Liv, who naturally replied with: *Got lost, huh?* as if he'd just failed to follow the directions properly. Then she sent GPS coordinates along with: *I hear G. Going to him now.*

Patrick texted back for her to wait. No reply to that one. She'd spotted Gabriel and nothing else mattered. Worse than starry-eyed teenagers, both of them.

He reached what was, according to his GPS app, the correct location. And there was no sign of Gabriel or Liv. He sent texts to both. Neither answered. So he started wandering about, looking and listening, soon as lost as if he'd been pixie-led himself.

When he turned down the next street, he finally caught the sound of Liv's distant voice.

"Hey, there," she was saying. "Did the pixie escape?"

"Pixie?" Gabriel said.

"Uh, yeah. The one you were guarding?"

"I don't know what you're talking about, Olivia."

Patrick swore under his breath. The pixie had cast her befuddlement magic on Gabriel and escaped. He looked for any sign of the fae, hoping her hunger for entertainment would outweigh her common sense, and she'd circle back to watch the fun.

But there was no sign of the pixie.

He continued toward Liv's and Gabriel's voices, and he was just about to round the corner when he caught what sounded like a titter. He stopped mid-step. He could sense her there, just ahead, so he crept along the wall and peered around the corner. Behind a dumpster, the pixie crouched, her attention on Liv and Gabriel.

Completely focused on the drama unfolding down the alley.

Patrick smiled.

He took a careful step, easing past—

Something moved beside the pixie. Patrick flung himself back around the corner. Then he peered out to see a male pixie crouched next to the female.

Two of them? Couldn't warn me about that, Gabriel?

Patrick shook his head. No matter. He could handle a couple of pixies, particularly when they were so enrapt in the scene up ahead.

"What are you talking about?" Liv was saying. "Fix what?"

Patrick had been ignoring their conversation. Now Gabriel was saying, again, that he didn't know what Liv was talking about. Patrick watched the pixies, timing his attack.

"You just said you had an hour to fix it," she said. "What does—?" She stopped, as if the realization hit her at the same time it did Patrick. As he whispered, *"Cach,"* she echoed it in English.

"Okay," Liv said. "You've been infected with pixie dust. We can handle this. One hour, huh?" She muttered under her breath, "Couldn't get the usual forty-eight, could you? Gabriel Walsh requires a real challenge."

"Olivia, I have no idea—"

"Yeah, yeah, you don't know what I'm talking about. Just hold tight. We'll get this...Gabriel?"

"Yes?"

A thud. Then Liv's voice. "What the hell? Get your—"

Another thump. Patrick ran to the corner and swung around it to see Gabriel there with his hands wrapped around Olivia's neck.

TWENTY-SIX

GABRIEL

GABRIEL HAD often heard the phrase "wanting to throttle" someone. Longing to put your hands around a person's neck and squeeze. It was, he presumed, an expression of frustration rather than an actual desire to kill. Normal people didn't smile when they said they wanted to shoot someone or bash their head in. They would, however, chuckle or roll their eyes when expressing a desire to strangle.

When Olivia texted him this suggestion, she'd even acknowledged that. *Pretend to strangle me. I'm sure you've wanted to do it often enough LOL.*

Except he hadn't. Any frustration he'd felt was exasperation, usually when she did something reckless, and it would hardly make sense to have the urge to kill someone because she was doing something that could get her killed.

Olivia, though, had likely battled the impulse to strangle *him*. Throttle some sense into him—that's how she'd put it. Understandable. But he'd never had that frustration with her. Even when she'd suggested he feign strangulation, he'd wanted to text back and say no, he'd rather not. He'd refrained only because he recognized that this was the best plan.

So he put his hands around her neck and squeezed, and it was one of the most difficult things he'd done in his life.

He had no issue with violence—that was the language of the streets. This was different. He put his hands around Olivia's neck, and he heard the pixie's words again, about fixing the problem, and it didn't matter if there was not one cell in his body that believed killing Olivia would fix anything in his life, that was still what this felt like. The culmination of all the tumult she'd brought into his world, twisted into a nightmare where he put his hands around her neck and squeezed until he was free.

It didn't matter that his hands barely cinched her neck. Didn't matter that she snuck a smile at him before she closed her eyes. That she stuck her tongue out the corner of her mouth, faking comic-level strangulation. That she did not tense, even for a second.

She trusted him.

Olivia let him put his hands around her neck, knowing the pixie had tried to convince him to kill her and trusting that he would not.

He didn't deserve that trust. Had not earned it. Wasn't sure he wanted the responsibility of it.

But it wasn't a matter of what *he* wanted. One didn't ask for trust. One received it as a gift. Olivia gave him hers, and he *did* want it. Any thoughts to the contrary arose from fear—the terror that he could not live up to the responsibility of her trust and therefore it was safest to refuse it.

He might not like even pretending to throttle her, but he did, gritting his teeth and carrying through with the plan and—

"Gabriel!" a voice shouted, and he did not need to wonder who that was. Nor did Olivia, her green eyes flying open in a death-glare aimed in the intruder's direction, as her lips formed his name: "Patrick."

Of course it was Patrick. Doing exactly what he did best: interfering. The bòcan shouted for Gabriel to stop as he raced forward, and the pixies launched themselves at him, taking him down.

"Just keep going," Olivia whispered, which was rather like carrying on a stage play while a riot erupted in the audience.

Patrick had come to their rescue. Damn him.

This was precisely what they had tried to avoid, ignoring his texts, giving him false directions and GPS coordinates. Gabriel would pretend to kill Olivia, and then once the pixies were convinced of success, they'd turn the tables. If they needed Patrick's help then, he would be within shouting distance. They did not, however, actually want him on the scene. And yet here he was, brawling with pixies.

Damnably inconvenient.

Gabriel glanced over at the fight.

"Just hold on," Olivia whispered. "I think I'm dead now. Lower me to the ground and keep your back to them…"

As he lowered her limp body, she kept her eyes open just enough to watch the fight.

"Okay," she whispered. "They're not paying any attention to us. So at the count of three…we run like hell and leave Patrick to his fate."

When Gabriel didn't respond, she sighed. "It was worth a shot. Fine. At the count of three, we rescue the damn bòcan. I've got the pixie-chick. You get the guy. Now, as I count down, start retreating, keeping your back to them, attention on my dead body, horrified by what you've done…"

He complied, ignoring the fact that he was backing *toward* a fight when he struggled to even sit in a restaurant without putting his back to a wall. Olivia was watching out for him, and he trusted her. Unquestioningly.

She counted down, and when she reached one, he wheeled and sprang. He grabbed the male pixie by the shoulders, yanking him off Patrick. They went down fighting. Which was not how this encounter was supposed to go at all. The plan was to resolve it with trickery, not violence. But Patrick had ruined that, and as Gabriel heard his suit jacket tear, he made a mental note that it would definitely be going on the bòcan's bill.

Gabriel subdued the male pixie. By then the female realized what was happening. She let out an inhuman squeal and charged in to save her mate. A shot from Olivia's gun stopped her.

The pixie looked at the gun, and then at the hole in the wall above her head.

"That was the warning shot," Olivia said. "The next one will be about a foot lower. And, in case you're wondering, yes, the bullets are cold iron. Patrick? Could you take that guy? He's bleeding all over Gabriel's shirt."

The male pixie gnashed his teeth, but Gabriel kept him pinned, moving off him only once Patrick had him secured.

"Okay, pixies," Olivia said. "You have the right—no, actually, the obligation to remain silent. Anything you say will definitely be used against you…"

❧

GABRIEL watched as Olivia rose from her perch on a gravestone. "Okay, it's nearly dawn, and I think we can leave. Looks like pixie-chick's curse-removal worked. Christina's gone, hopefully gone to wherever she should be." She brushed off her jeans. "So, how do you feel?"

"Fine."

She peered at him. "Are you sure?"

He was. The pixie's magic had failed because Gabriel knew he was lost. He knew he had to find his way back. And he knew he couldn't do that in one hour...or in forty-eight. He might want to mend things with Olivia quickly, but this wasn't like his other betrayals. He'd hurt her too much for a speedy fix.

As they started walking, she yawned, and he said, "Rest tomorrow. Take Monday off, too."

She tensed. "No, I—"

"That isn't a hint not to come back to work."

"I know. I just..."

"The last time I told you that, it wasn't a threat. It was me being, as you'd say, pissy. And, yes, it was a warning. An inexcusable warning, which I regret, and for which I am apologizing." He glanced over at her. "I would never have fired you. I ought not to have said or done anything to suggest I might. I'm sorry, and it won't happen again."

They took a few steps in silence, and he could sense her clamping her jaw shut against a response.

"Let me rephrase that," he said. "I promise I will endeavor to ensure it does not happen again, and if it does, you can be assured I do not mean it, and that if I continue in that vein, I should understand that you will find employment elsewhere, which I wouldn't want. Is that better?"

She forced a smile. "It is. You don't do well with absolutes, Gabriel."

"I know." He steeled himself to continue. "But when I say I don't want to lose you, Olivia, I do mean that." He let the declaration hang there for exactly three seconds before he had to add, "Where else would I find an investigator to work with me?"

She laughed and shook her head.

"I know you said you feel fine," she said after a few steps, "but can I ask you a favor?"

"Anything."

"Monday night, let's work late. Until about eleven p.m."

"Forty-eight hours post-pixies?"

"Humor me, okay?" She leaned her head against his shoulder for just a second. "I wouldn't want to lose you, either." A two-second pause. "Where else would I find someone to hire me?"

He gave her a smile for that, and they continued out of the cemetery.